VICTOR HUGO'S

LES
MISÉRABLES

A GRAPHIC NOVEL

BY LUCIANO SARACINO &
FABIÁN MEZQUITA

STONE ARCH BOOKS
A CAPSTONE IMPRINT

Graphic Revolve: Classic Fiction is published by
Stone Arch Books
1710 Roe Crest Drive
North Mankato, Minnesota 56003
www.mycapstone.com

Cataloging-in-Publication Data is available on the Library of Congress website.
ISBN 978-1-4965-6111-4 (library binding)
ISBN 978-1-4965-6116-9 (paperback)
ISBN 978-1-4965-6120-6 (eBook PDF)

Summary: The ex-convict Jean Valjean vows to change his ways and to become a kind and respected man. But with the merciless Inspector Javert hunting him down, can Valjean ever truly escape his past, protect those he loves, and find redemption?

Author: Luciano Saracino
Illustrator: Fabián Mezquita

Translated into the English language by Trusted Translations.

Printed in the United States of America.
010764S18

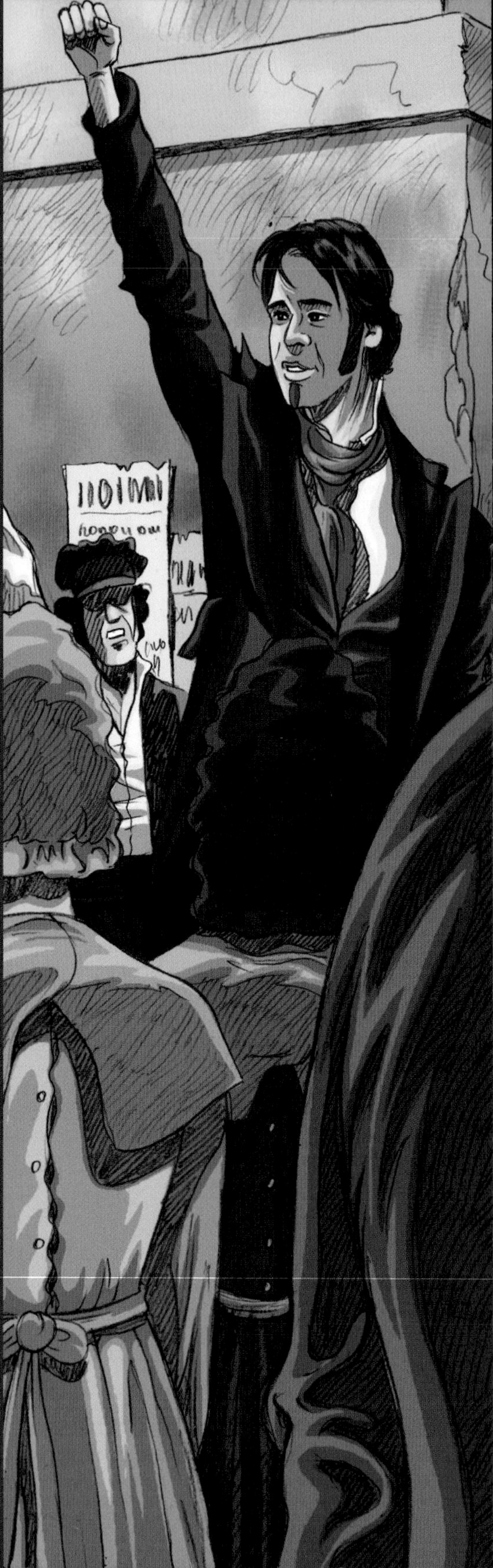

TABLE OF CONTENTS

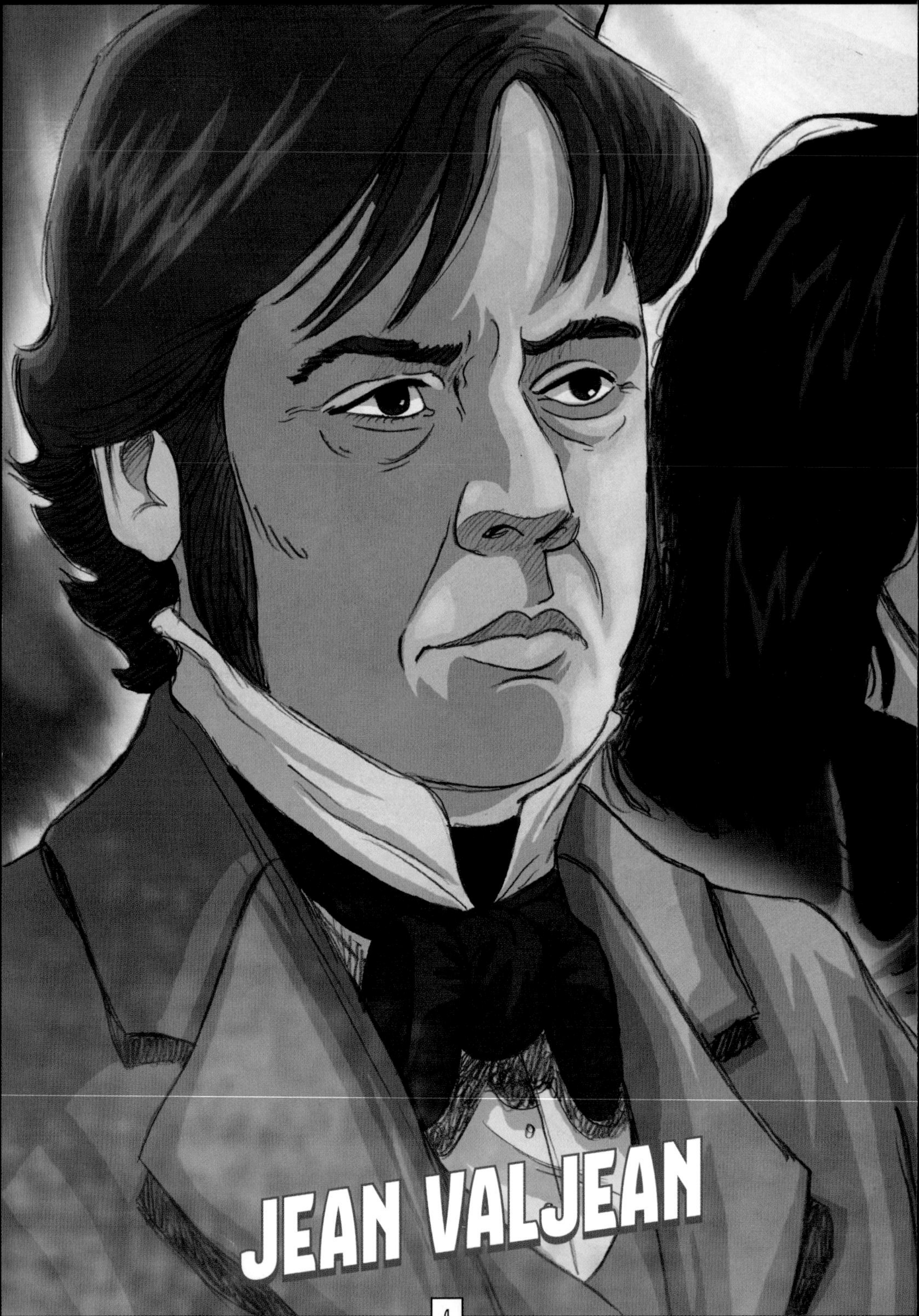
JEAN VALJEAN

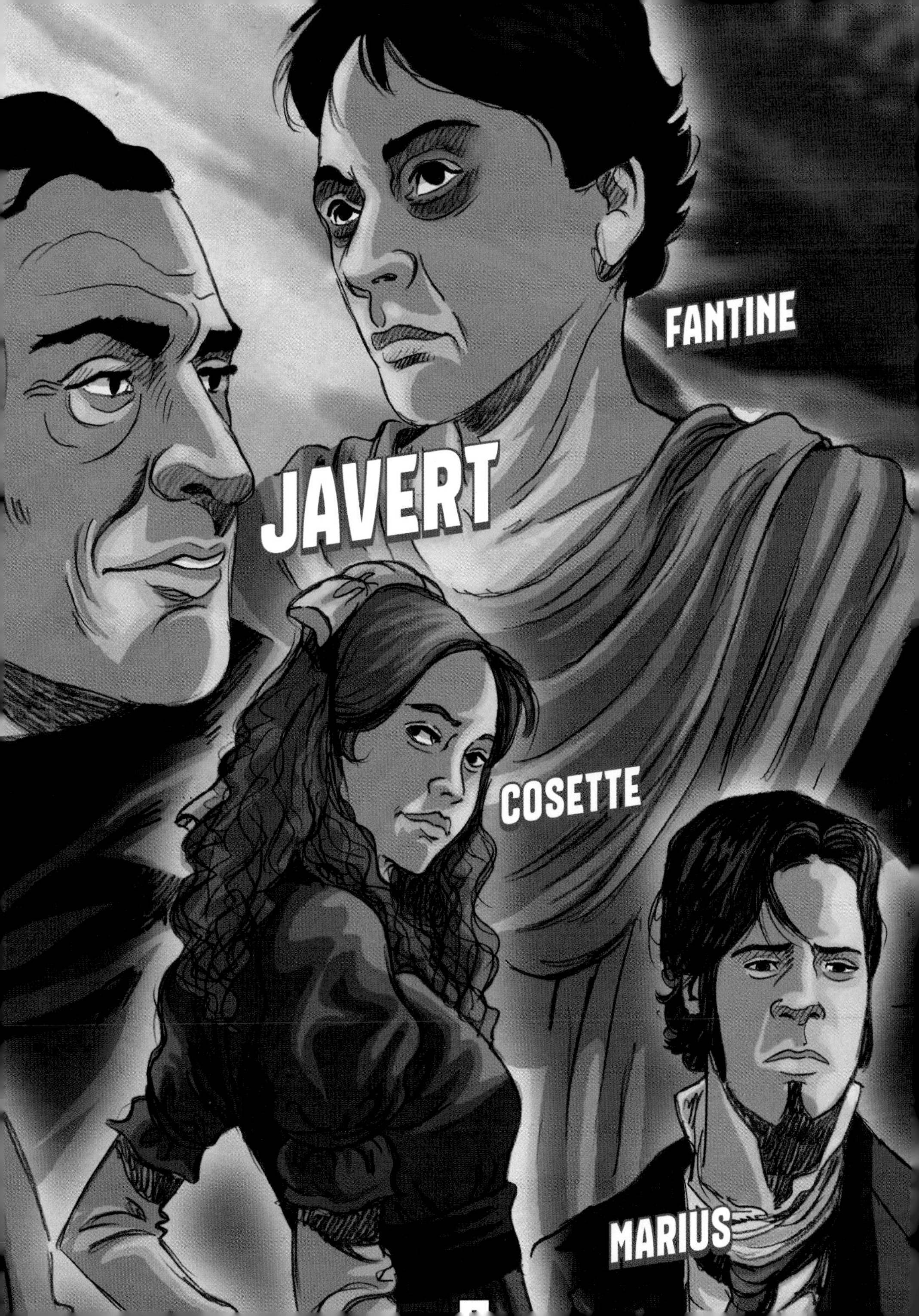
FANTINE
JAVERT
COSETTE
MARIUS

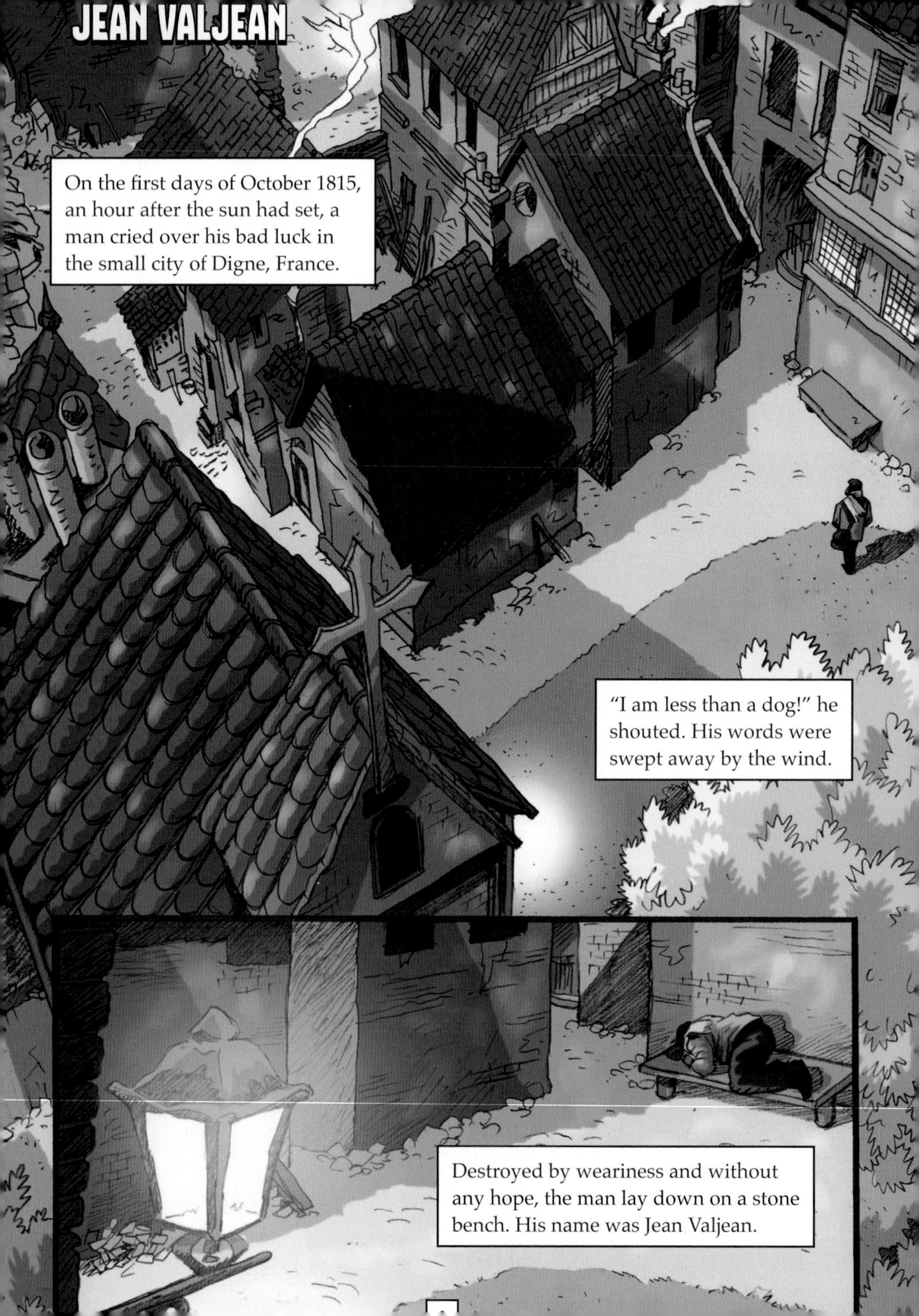
JEAN VALJEAN
On the first days of October 1815, an hour after the sun had set, a man cried over his bad luck in the small city of Digne, France.
"I am less than a dog!" he shouted. His words were swept away by the wind.
Destroyed by weariness and without any hope, the man lay down on a stone bench. His name was Jean Valjean.

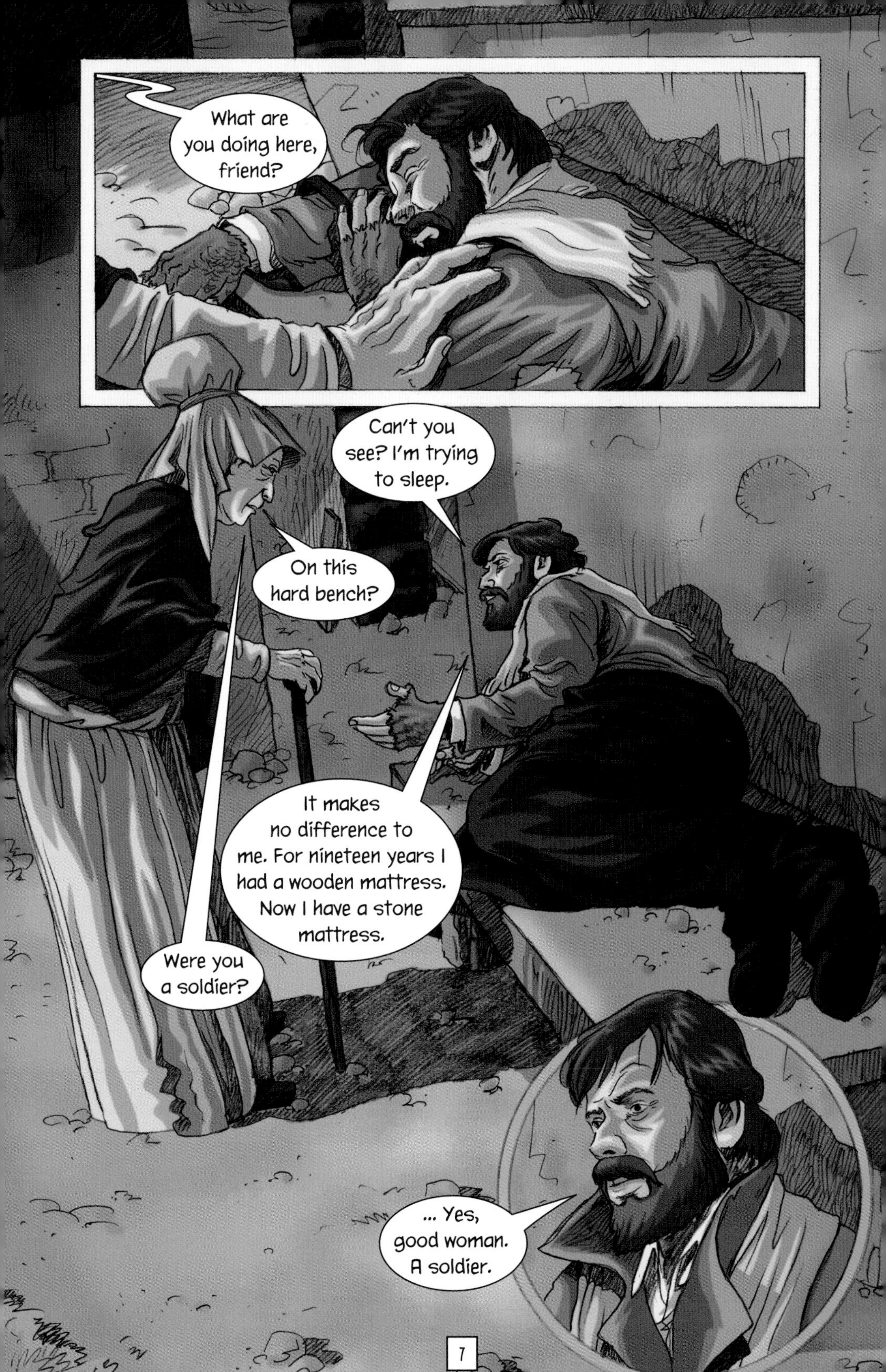
What are you doing here, friend?
Can't you see? I'm trying to sleep.
On this hard bench?
It makes no difference to me. For nineteen years I had a wooden mattress. Now I have a stone mattress.
Were you a soldier?
... Yes, good woman. A soldier.

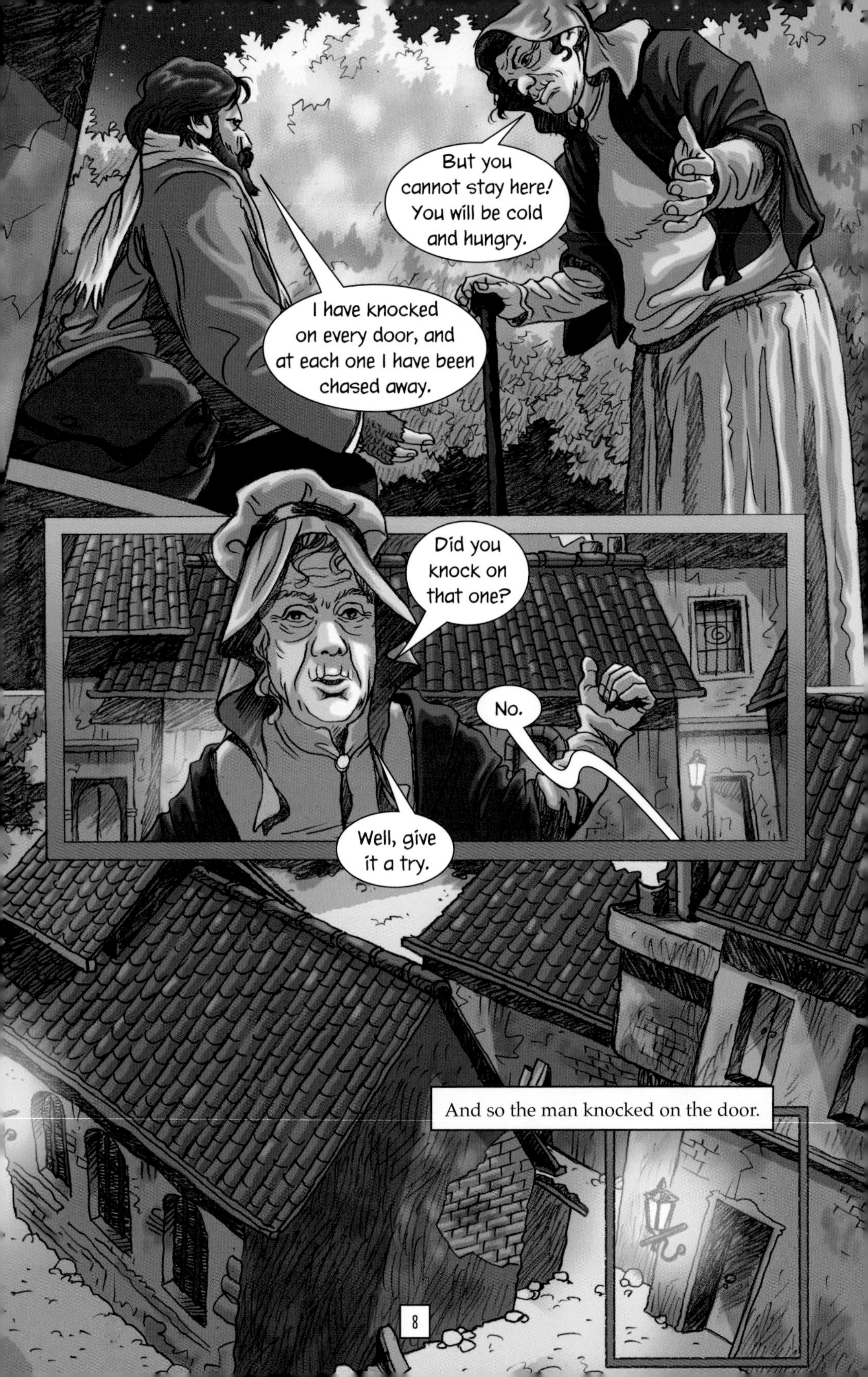
But you cannot stay here! You will be cold and hungry.
I have knocked on every door, and at each one I have been chased away.
Did you knock on that one?
No.
Well, give it a try.
And so the man knocked on the door.

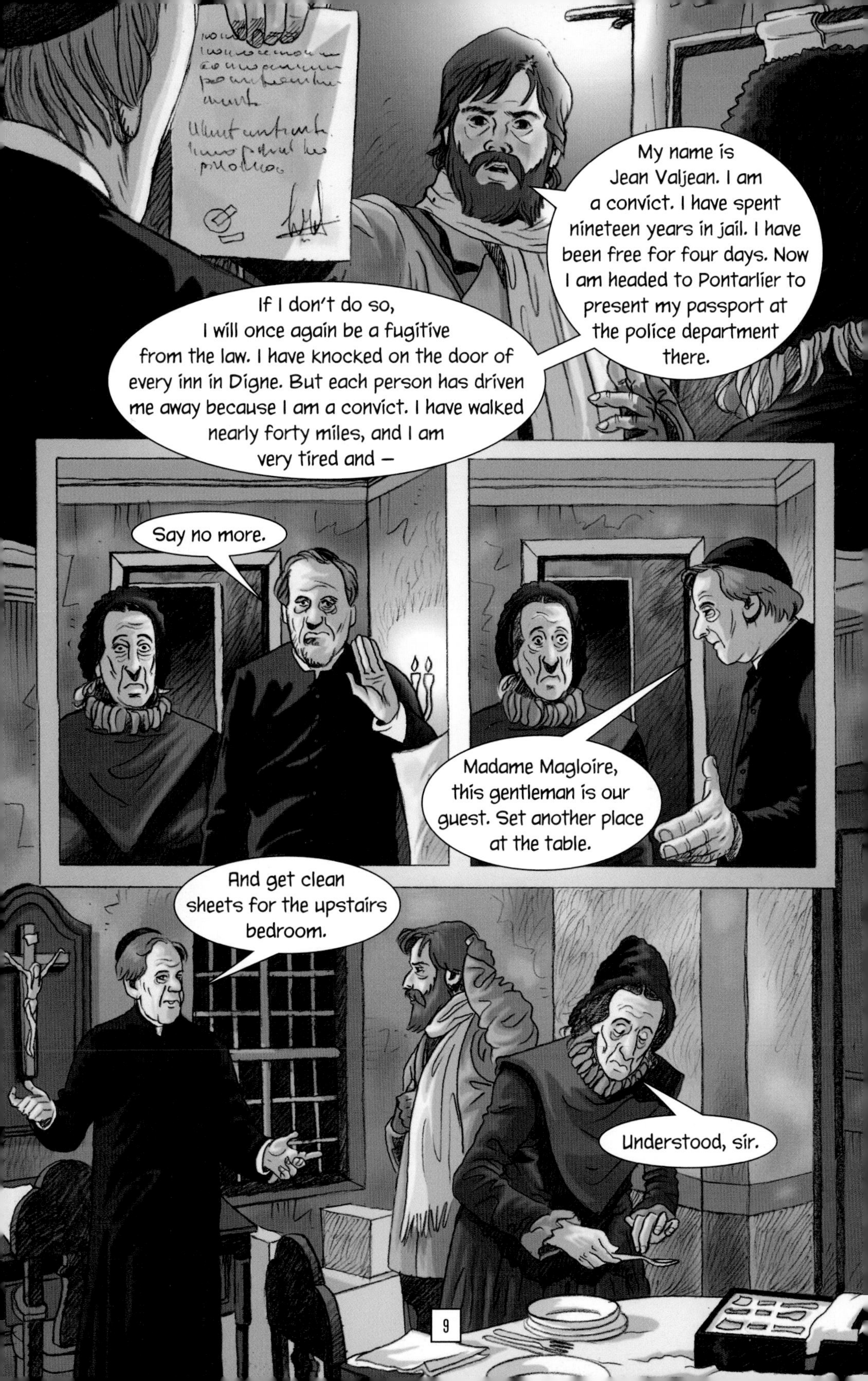
My name is Jean Valjean. I am a convict. I have spent nineteen years in jail. I have been free for four days. Now I am headed to Pontarlier to present my passport at the police department there.
If I don't do so, I will once again be a fugitive from the law. I have knocked on the door of every inn in Digne. But each person has driven me away because I am a convict. I have walked nearly forty miles, and I am very tired and —
Say no more.
Madame Magloire, this gentleman is our guest. Set another place at the table.
And get clean sheets for the upstairs bedroom.
Understood, sir.

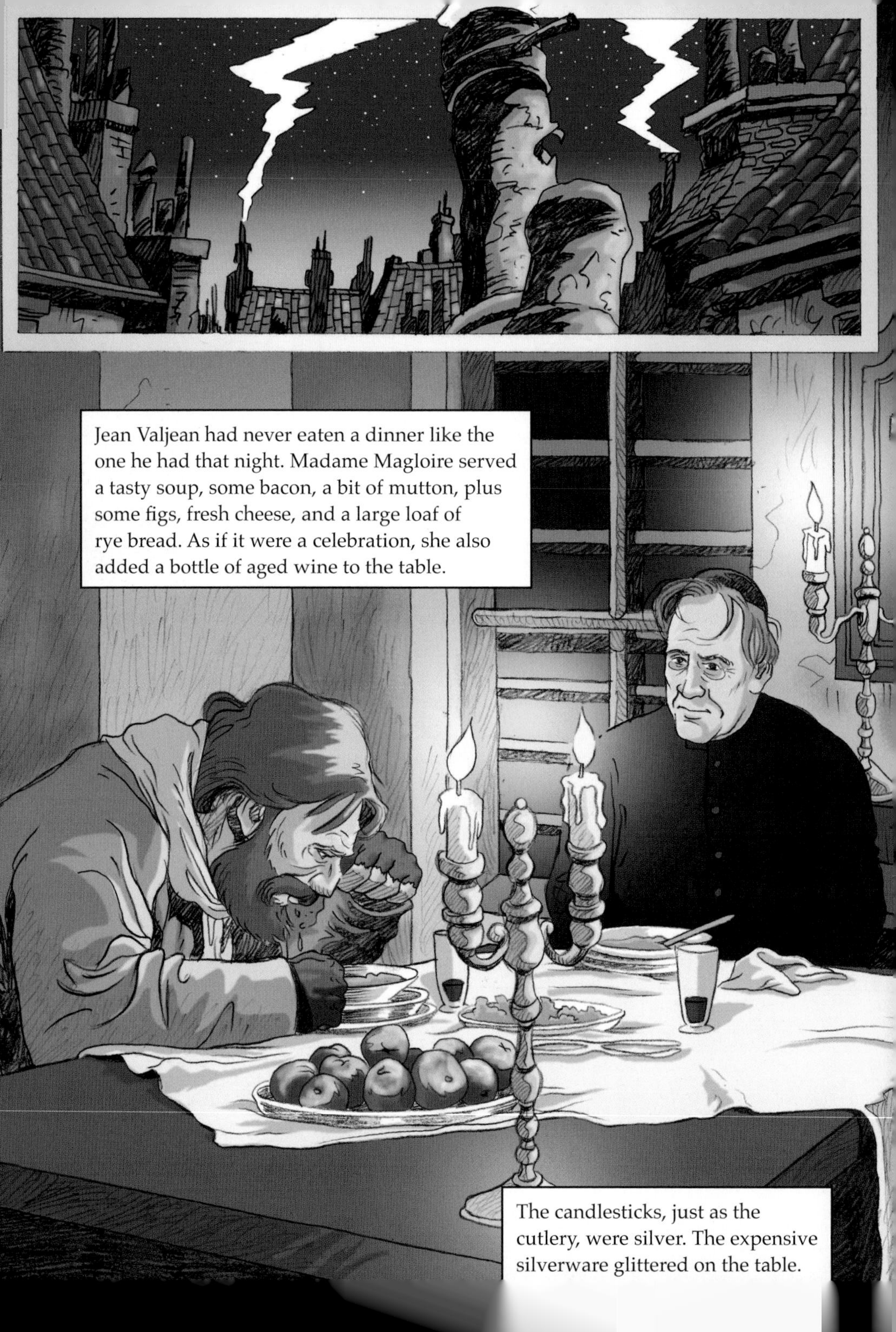
Jean Valjean had never eaten a dinner like the one he had that night. Madame Magloire served a tasty soup, some bacon, a bit of mutton, plus some figs, fresh cheese, and a large loaf of rye bread. As if it were a celebration, she also added a bottle of aged wine to the table.
The candlesticks, just as the cutlery, were silver. The expensive silverware glittered on the table.

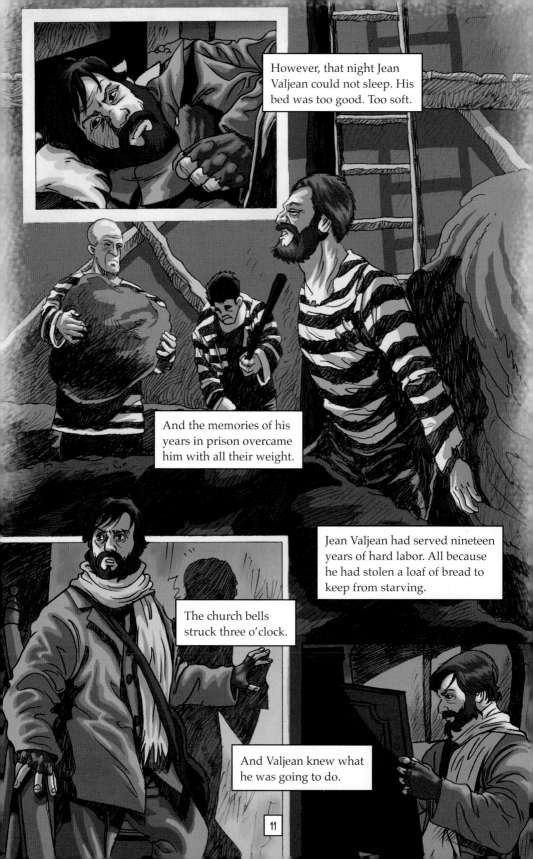

However, that night Jean Valjean could not sleep. His bed was too good. Too soft.

And the memories of his years in prison overcame him with all their weight.

Jean Valjean had served nineteen years of hard labor. All because he had stolen a loaf of bread to keep from starving.

The church bells struck three o'clock.

And Valjean knew what he was going to do.

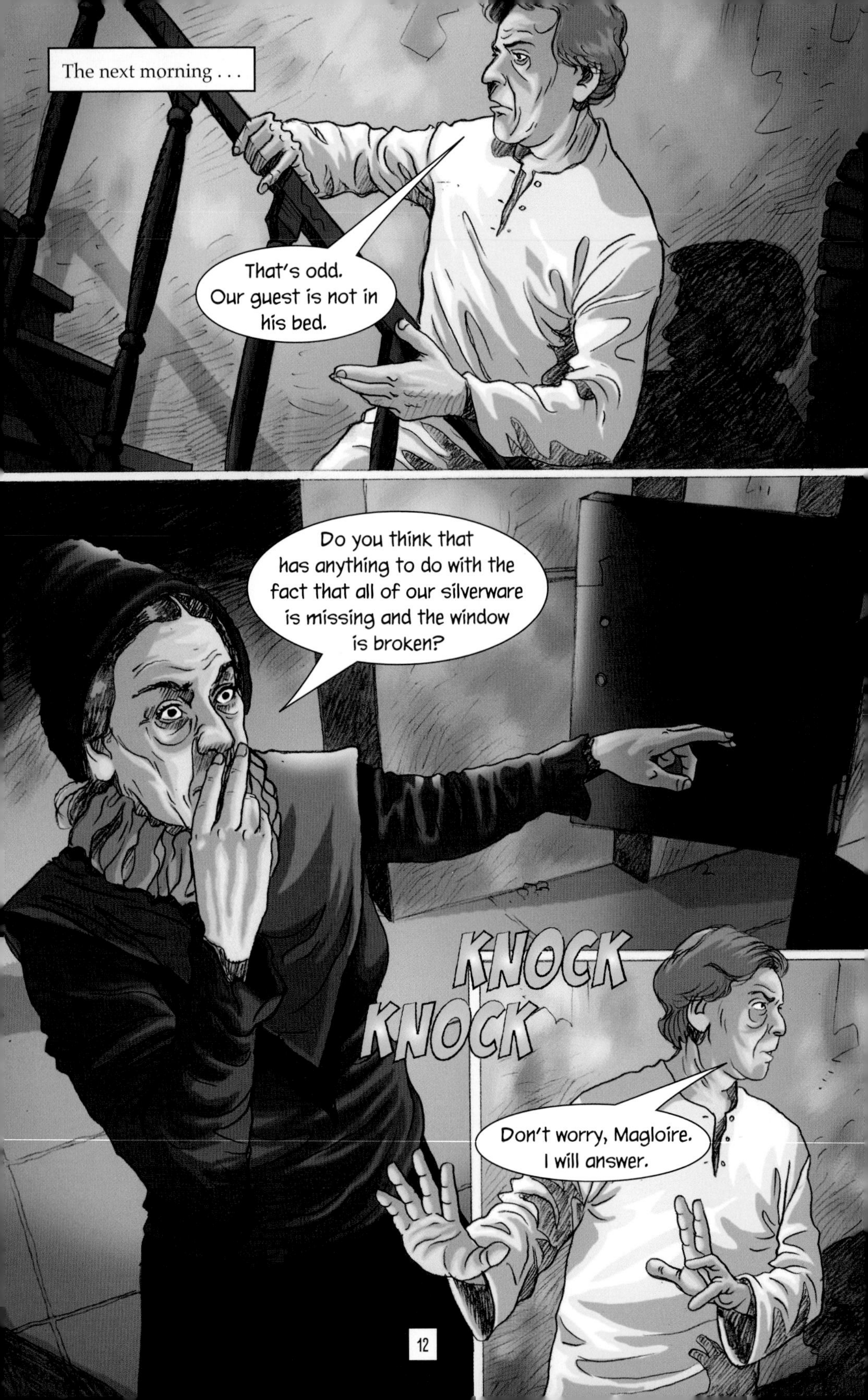
The next morning . . .
That's odd. Our guest is not in his bed.
Do you think that has anything to do with the fact that all of our silverware is missing and the window is broken?
KNOCK KNOCK
Don't worry, Magloire. I will answer.

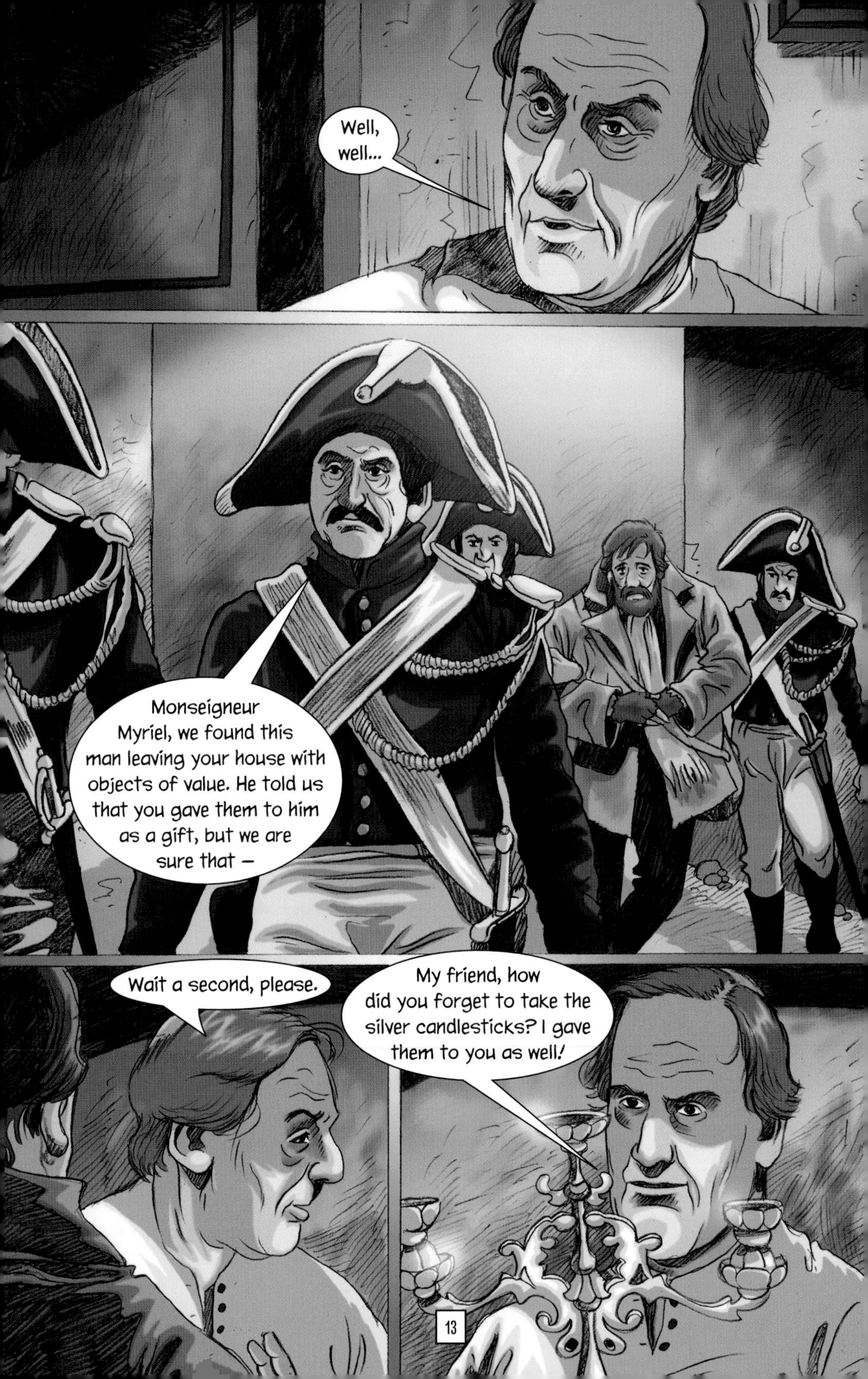
Well, well...
Monseigneur Myriel, we found this man leaving your house with objects of value. He told us that you gave them to him as a gift, but we are sure that –
Wait a second, please.
My friend, how did you forget to take the silver candlesticks? I gave them to you as well!

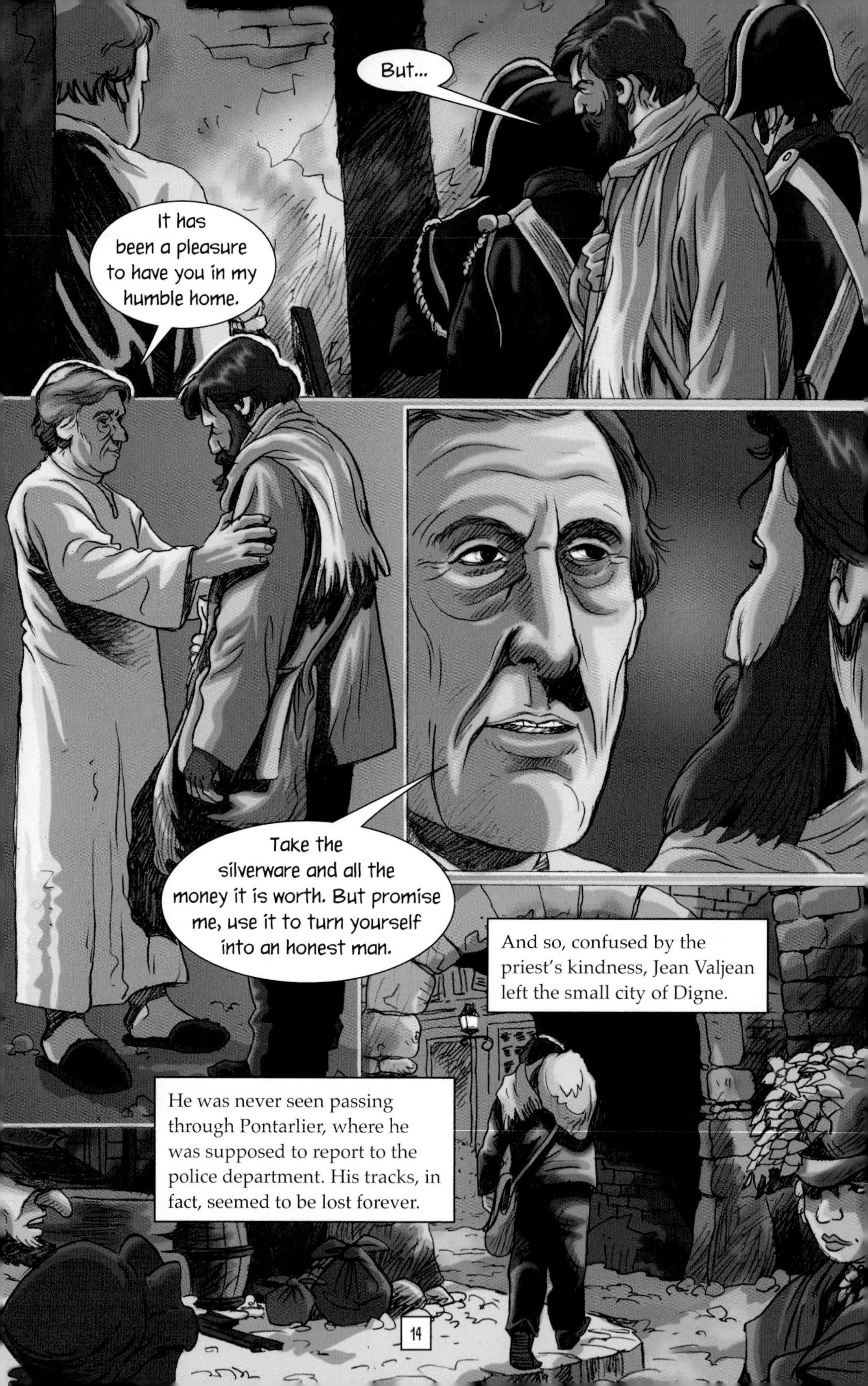
It has been a pleasure to have you in my humble home.
But...
Take the silverware and all the money it is worth. But promise me, use it to turn yourself into an honest man.
And so, confused by the priest's kindness, Jean Valjean left the small city of Digne.
He was never seen passing through Pontarlier, where he was supposed to report to the police department. His tracks, in fact, seemed to be lost forever.

CHAPTER 2
FANTINE

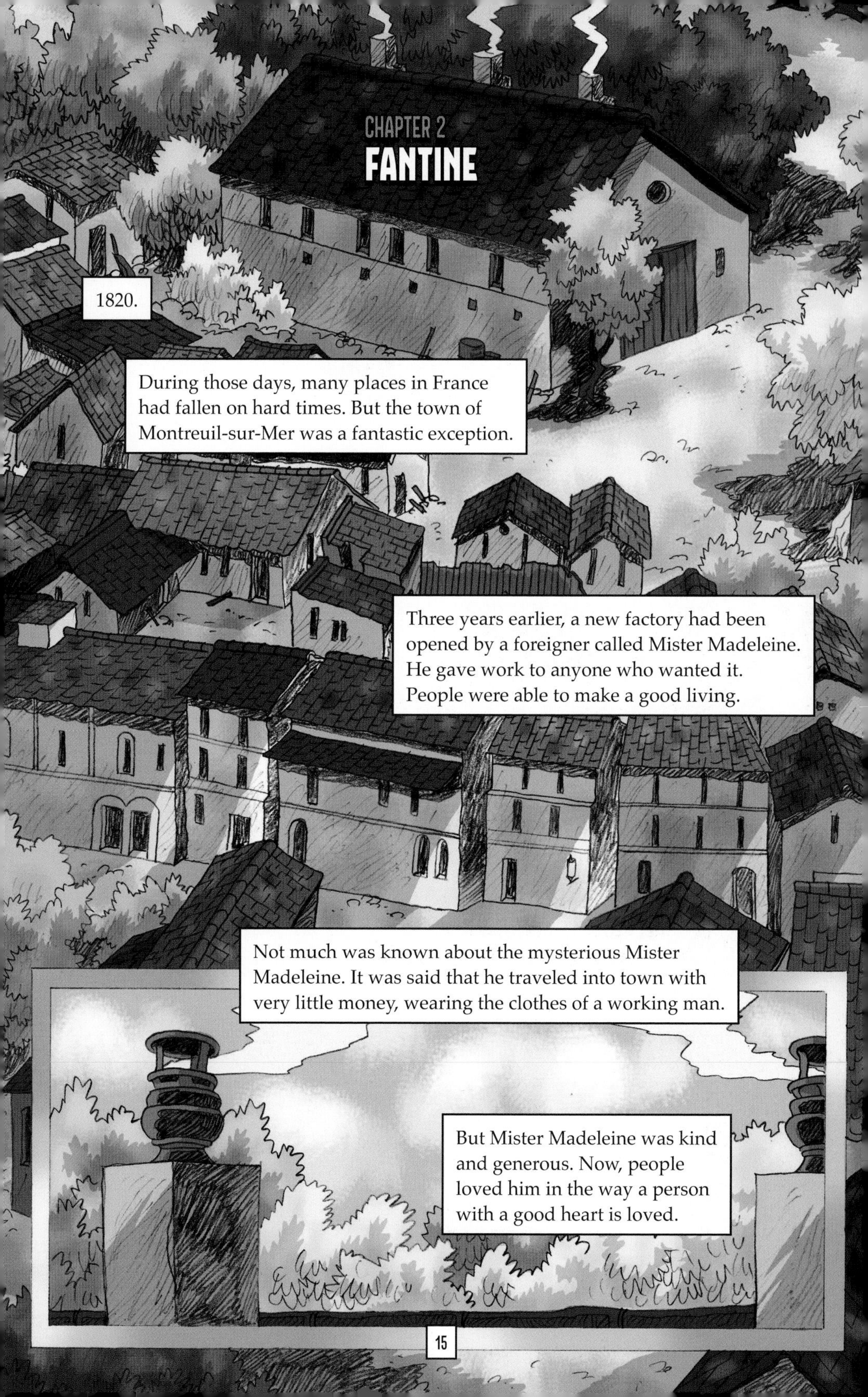
1820.
During those days, many places in France had fallen on hard times. But the town of Montreuil-sur-Mer was a fantastic exception.
Three years earlier, a new factory had been opened by a foreigner called Mister Madeleine. He gave work to anyone who wanted it. People were able to make a good living.
Not much was known about the mysterious Mister Madeleine. It was said that he traveled into town with very little money, wearing the clothes of a working man.
But Mister Madeleine was kind and generous. Now, people loved him in the way a person with a good heart is loved.

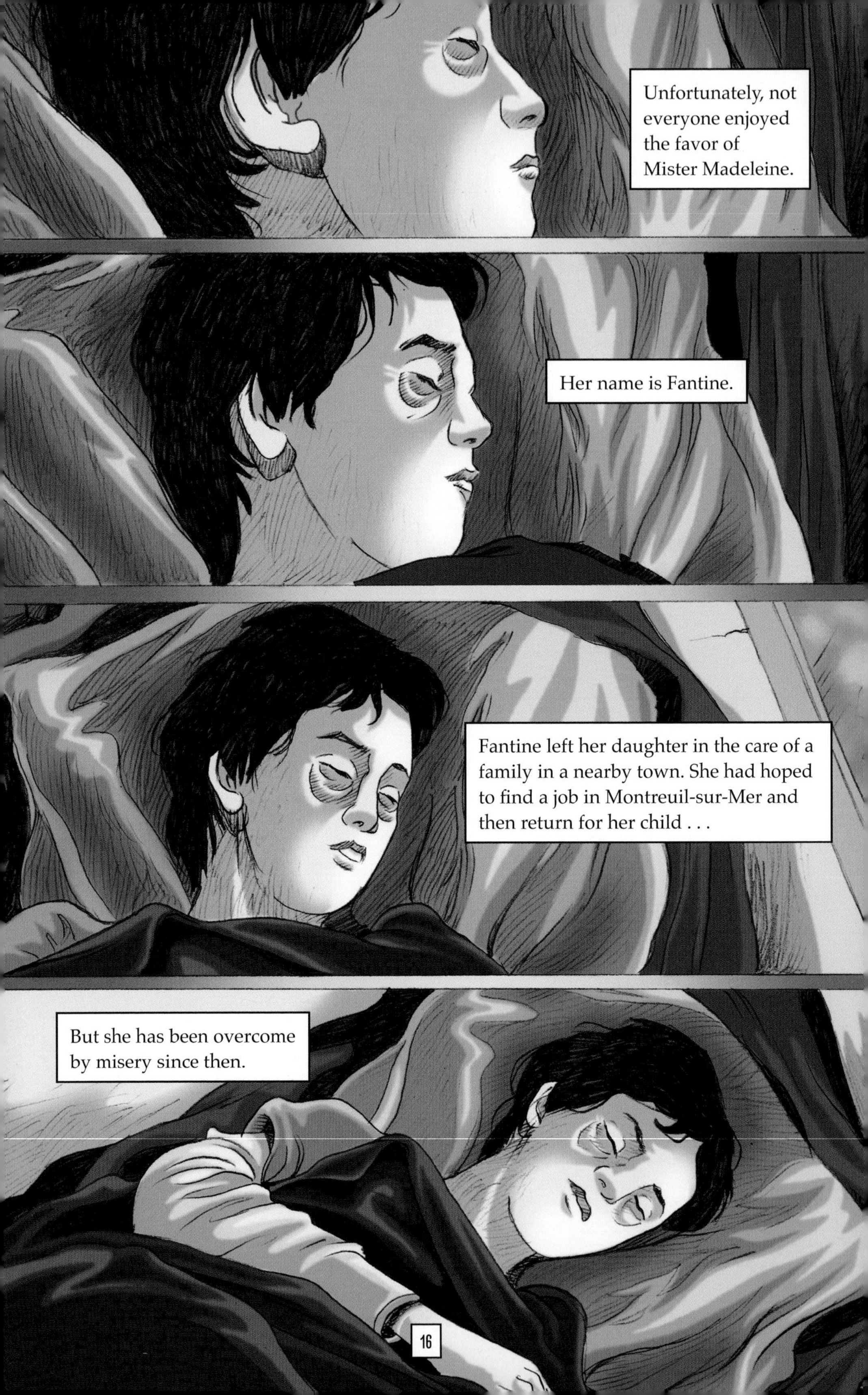
Unfortunately, not everyone enjoyed the favor of Mister Madeleine.
Her name is Fantine.
Fantine left her daughter in the care of a family in a nearby town. She had hoped to find a job in Montreuil-sur-Mer and then return for her child . . .
But she has been overcome by misery since then.

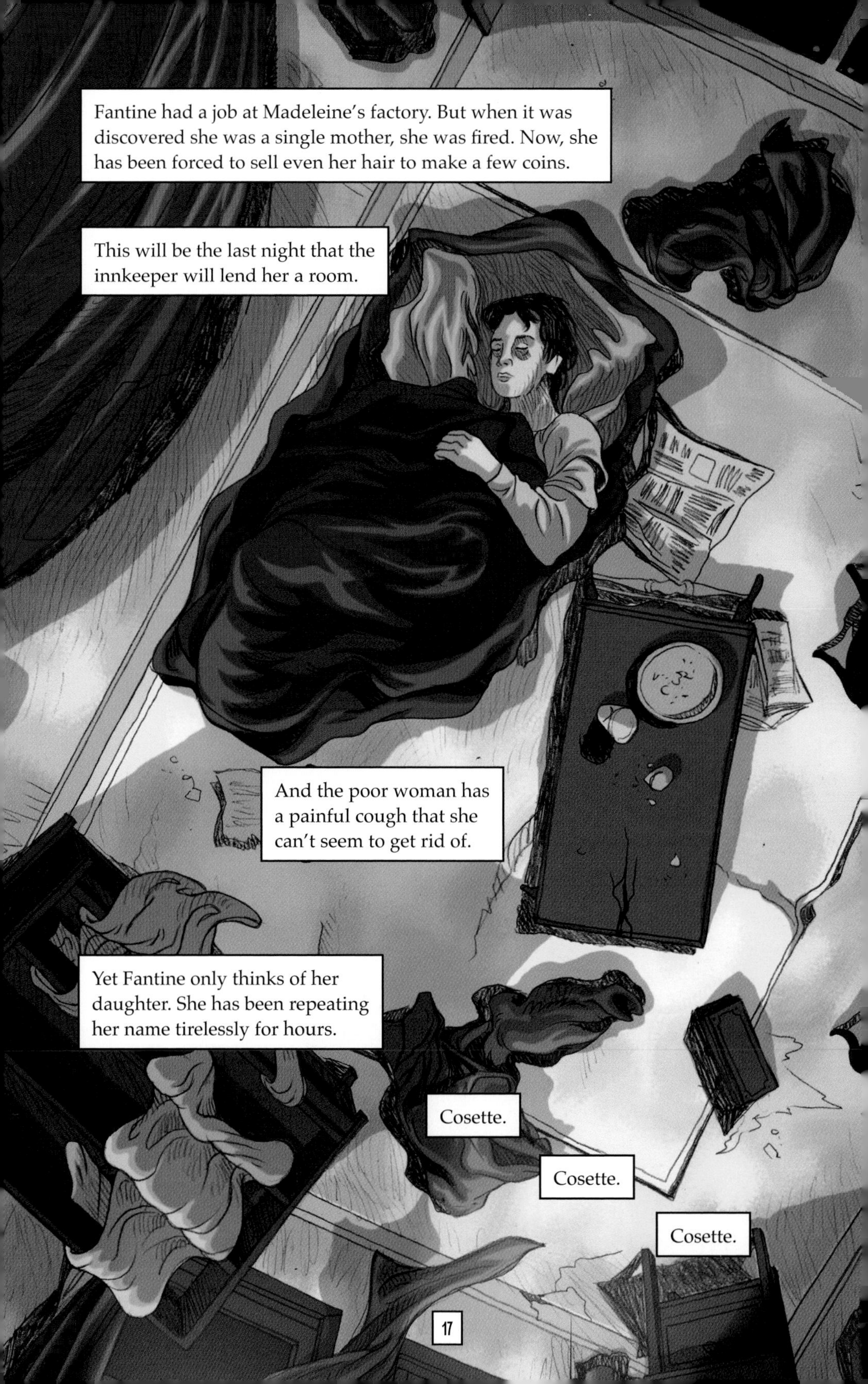
Fantine had a job at Madeleine's factory. But when it was discovered she was a single mother, she was fired. Now, she has been forced to sell even her hair to make a few coins.
This will be the last night that the innkeeper will lend her a room.
And the poor woman has a painful cough that she can't seem to get rid of.
Yet Fantine only thinks of her daughter. She has been repeating her name tirelessly for hours.
Cosette.
Cosette.
Cosette.

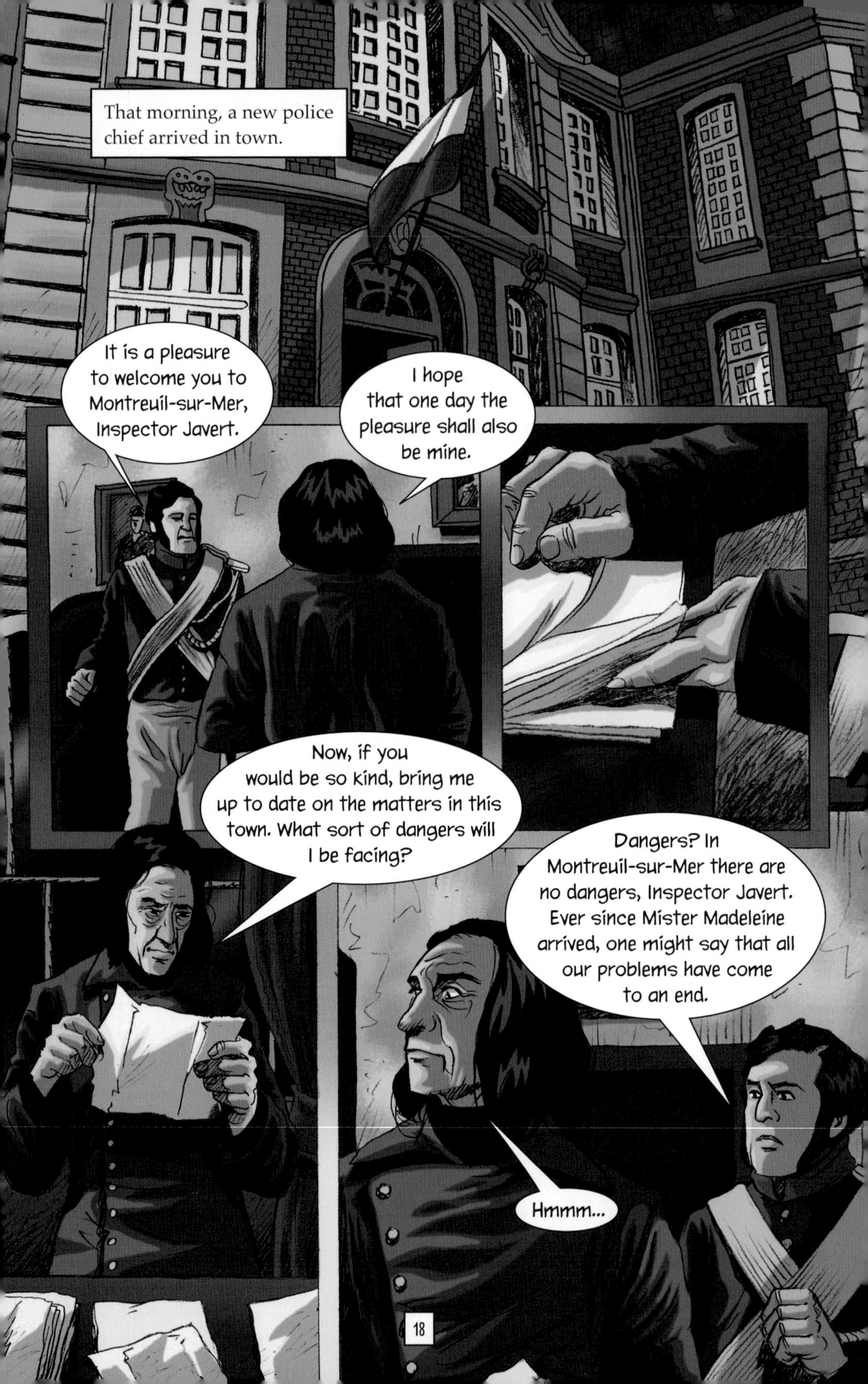

That morning, a new police chief arrived in town.
It is a pleasure to welcome you to Montreuil-sur-Mer, Inspector Javert.
I hope that one day the pleasure shall also be mine.
Now, if you would be so kind, bring me up to date on the matters in this town. What sort of dangers will I be facing?
Dangers? In Montreuil-sur-Mer there are no dangers, Inspector Javert. Ever since Mister Madeleine arrived, one might say that all our problems have come to an end.
Hmmm...

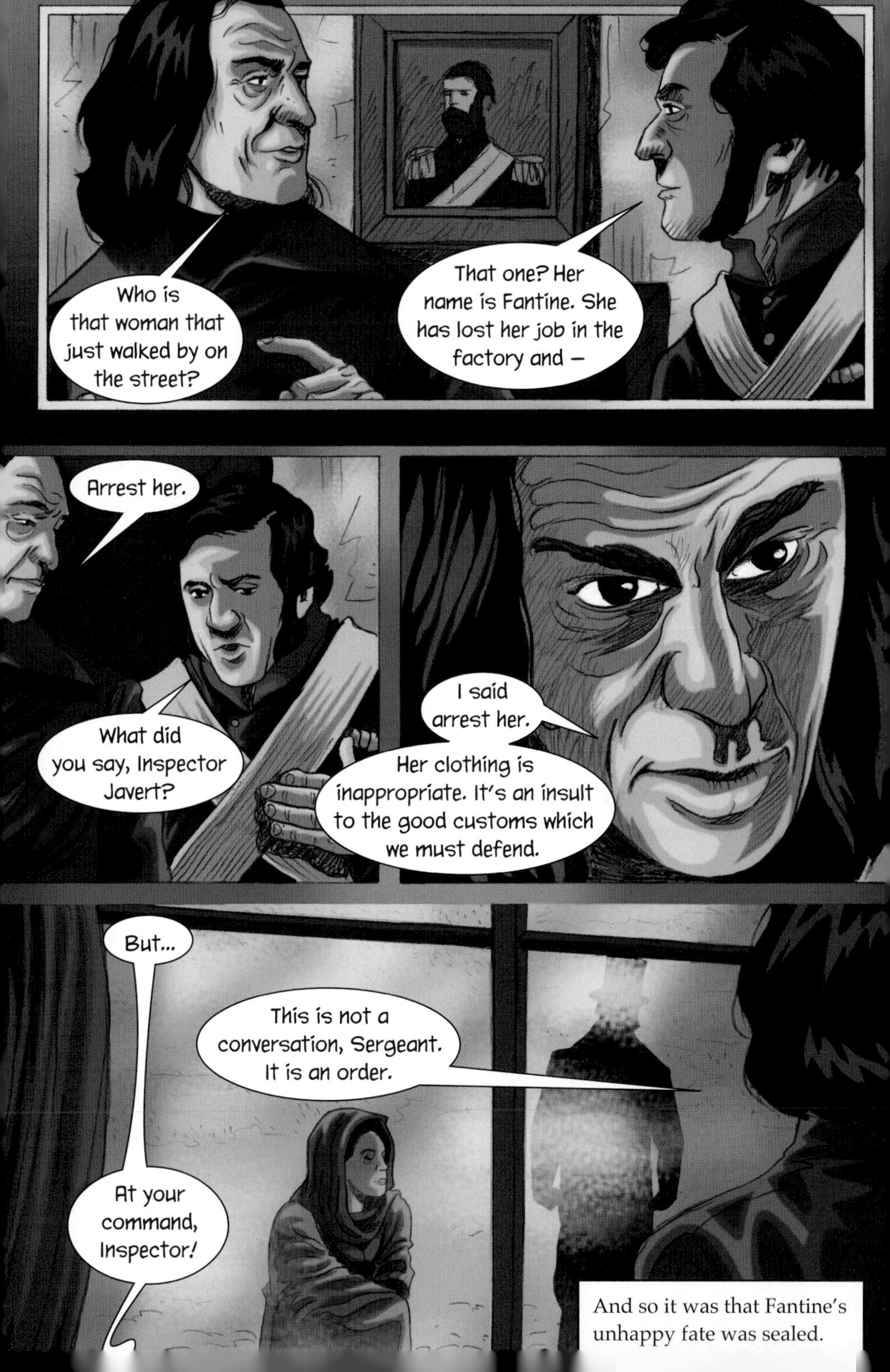
Who is that woman that just walked by on the street?
That one? Her name is Fantine. She has lost her job in the factory and —
Arrest her.
What did you say, Inspector Javert?
I said arrest her.
Her clothing is inappropriate. It's an insult to the good customs which we must defend.
But...
This is not a conversation, Sergeant. It is an order.
At your command, Inspector!
And so it was that Fantine's unhappy fate was sealed.

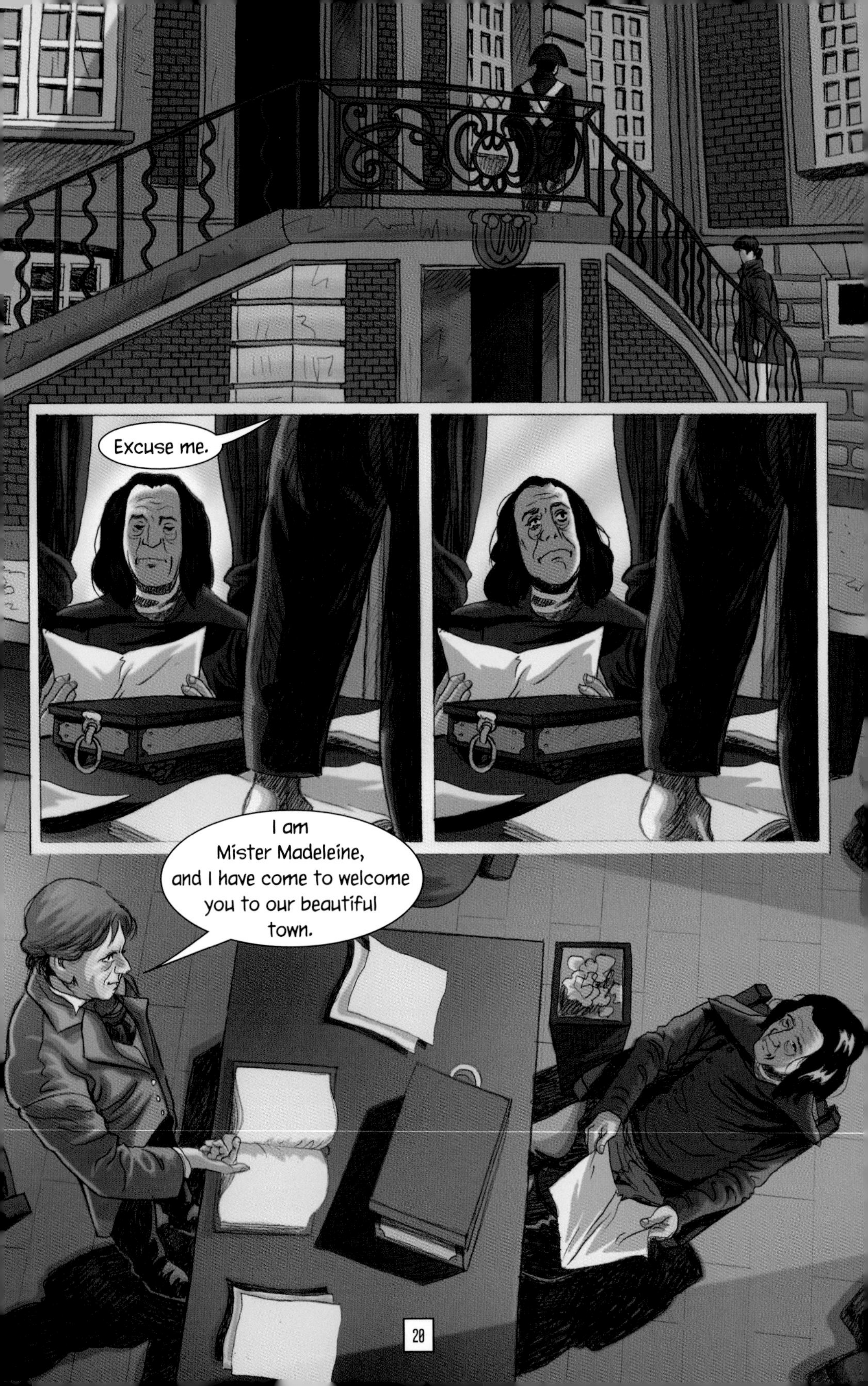
Excuse me.
I am Mister Madeleine, and I have come to welcome you to our beautiful town.

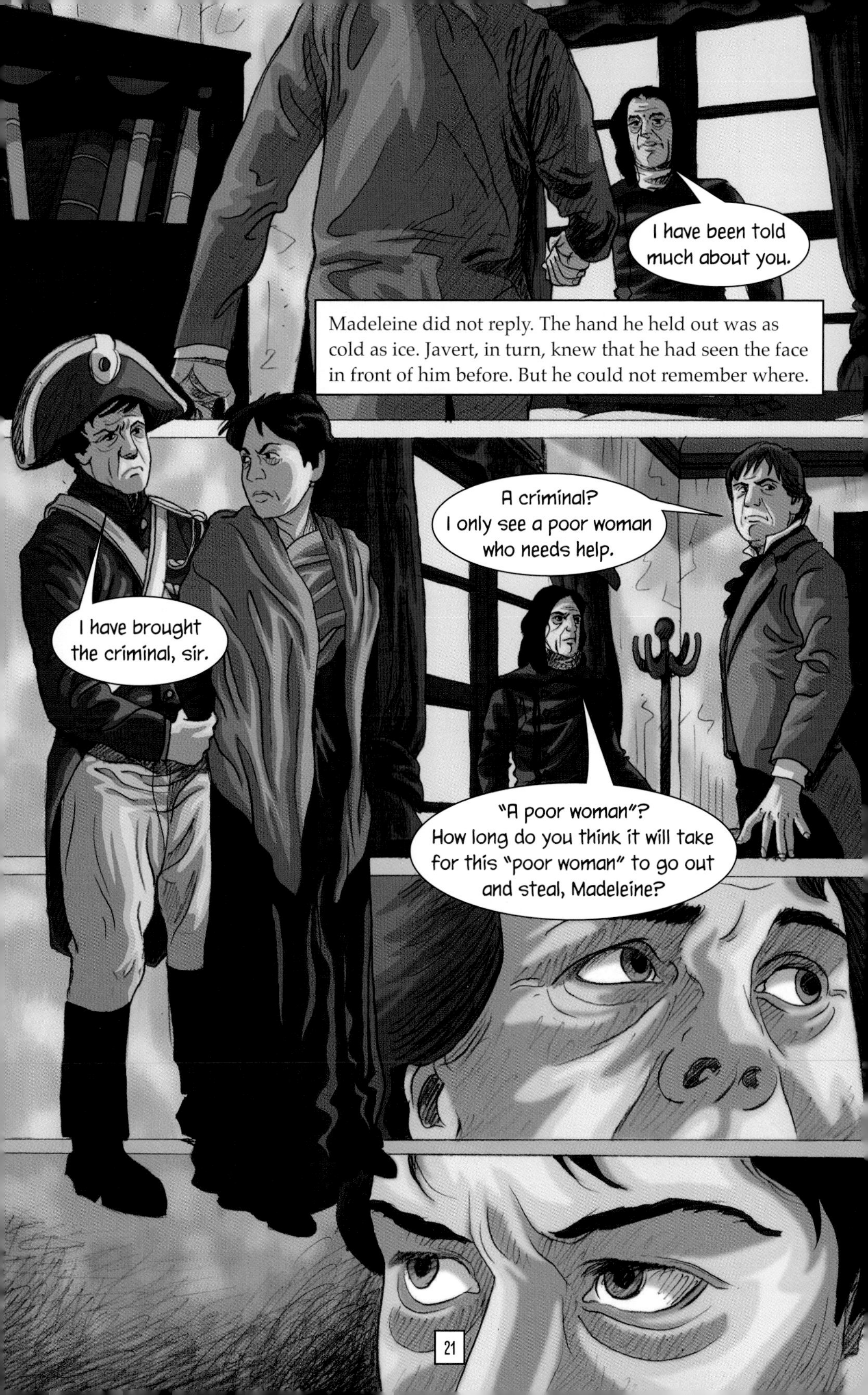

I have been told much about you.
Madeleine did not reply. The hand he held out was as cold as ice. Javert, in turn, knew that he had seen the face in front of him before. But he could not remember where.
I have brought the criminal, sir.
A criminal? I only see a poor woman who needs help.
"A poor woman"? How long do you think it will take for this "poor woman" to go out and steal, Madeleine?

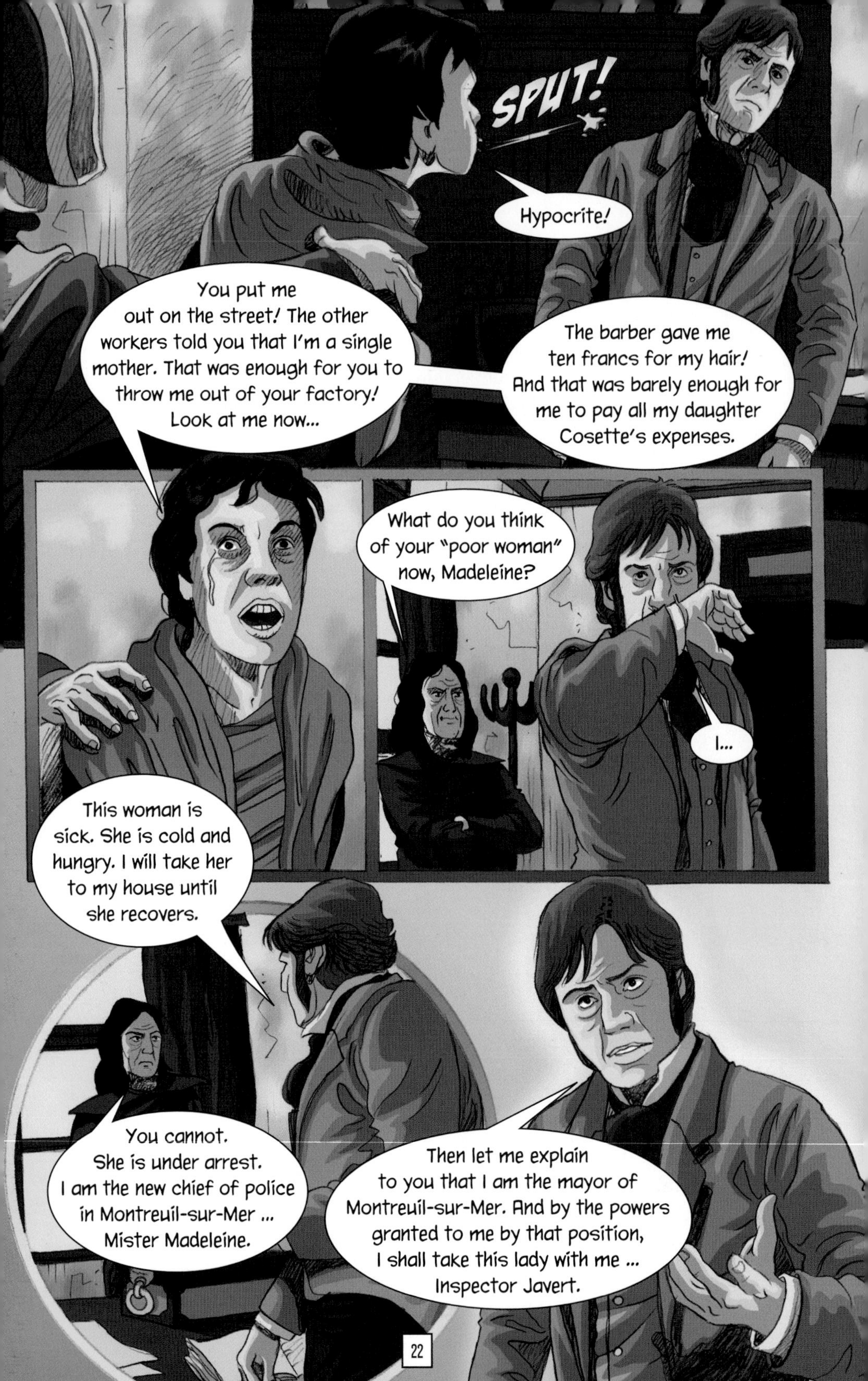
SPUT!
Hypocrite!
You put me out on the street! The other workers told you that I'm a single mother. That was enough for you to throw me out of your factory! Look at me now...
The barber gave me ten francs for my hair! And that was barely enough for me to pay all my daughter Cosette's expenses.
What do you think of your "poor woman" now, Madeleine?
I...
This woman is sick. She is cold and hungry. I will take her to my house until she recovers.
You cannot. She is under arrest. I am the new chief of police in Montreuil-sur-Mer ... Mister Madeleine.
Then let me explain to you that I am the mayor of Montreuil-sur-Mer. And by the powers granted to me by that position, I shall take this lady with me ... Inspector Javert.

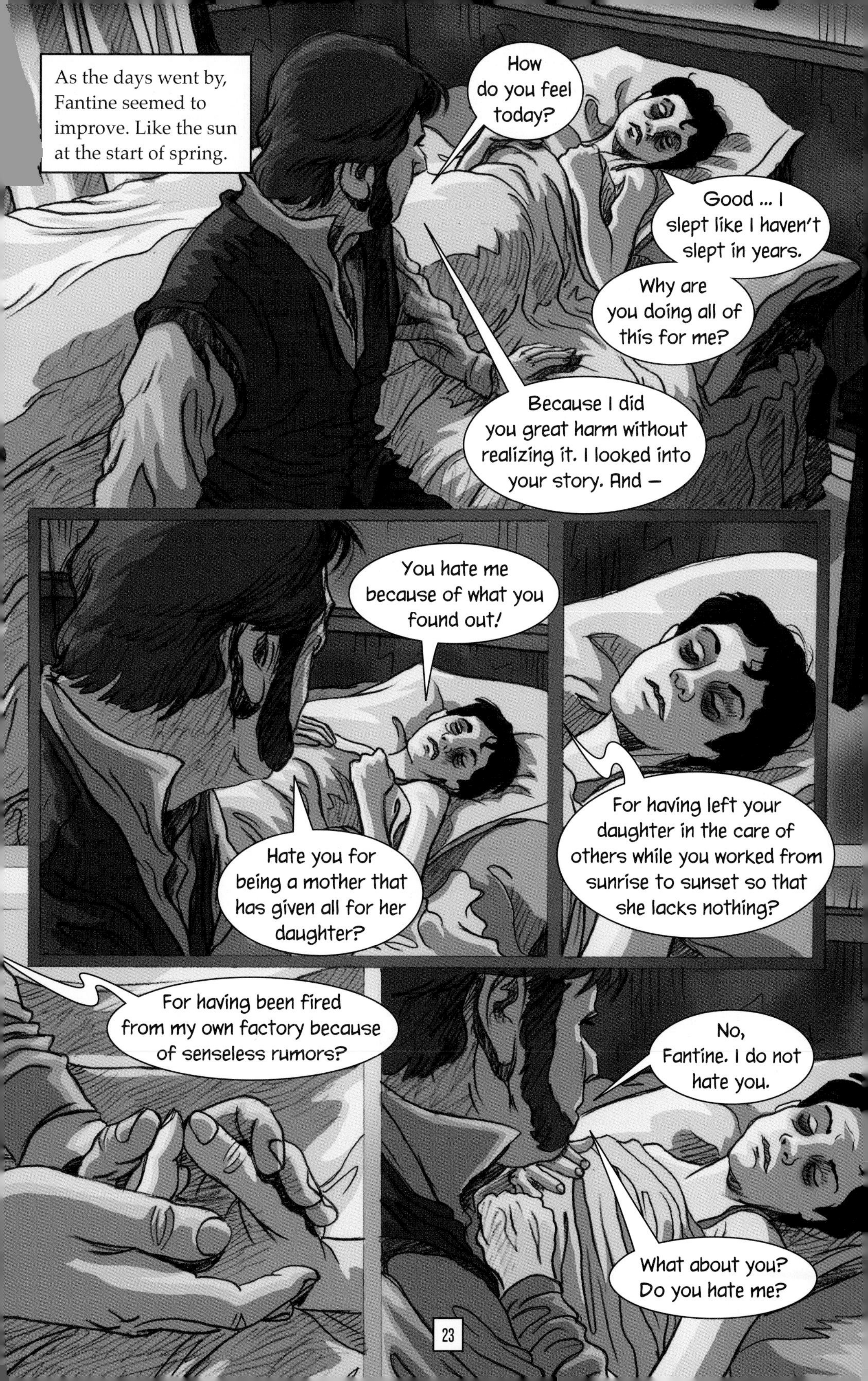
As the days went by, Fantine seemed to improve. Like the sun at the start of spring.
How do you feel today?
Good ... I slept like I haven't slept in years.
Why are you doing all of this for me?
Because I did you great harm without realizing it. I looked into your story. And —
You hate me because of what you found out!
Hate you for being a mother that has given all for her daughter?
For having left your daughter in the care of others while you worked from sunrise to sunset so that she lacks nothing?
For having been fired from my own factory because of senseless rumors?
No, Fantine. I do not hate you.
What about you? Do you hate me?

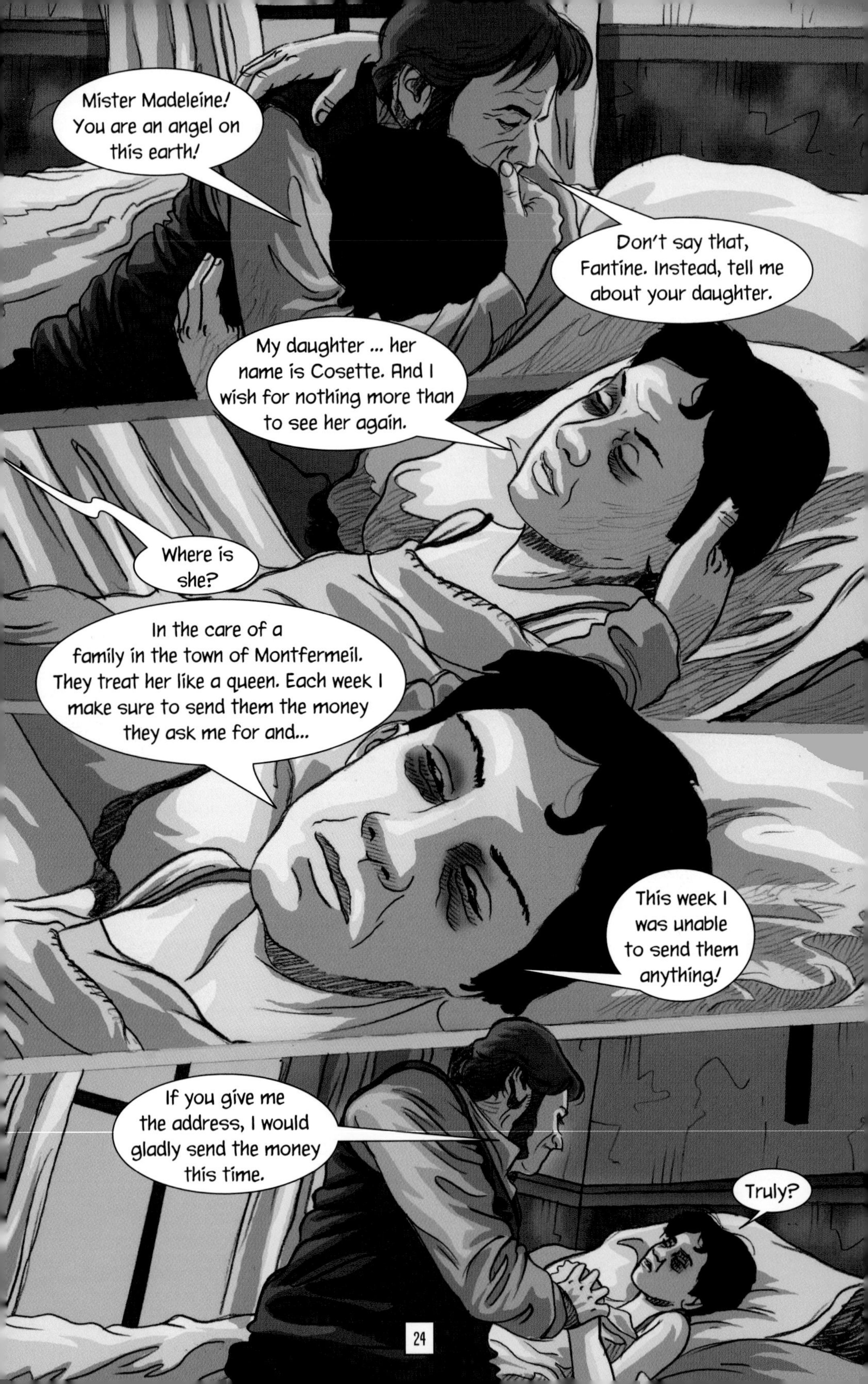
Mister Madeleine! You are an angel on this earth!
Don't say that, Fantine. Instead, tell me about your daughter.
My daughter ... her name is Cosette. And I wish for nothing more than to see her again.
Where is she?
In the care of a family in the town of Montfermeil. They treat her like a queen. Each week I make sure to send them the money they ask me for and...
This week I was unable to send them anything!
If you give me the address, I would gladly send the money this time.
Truly?

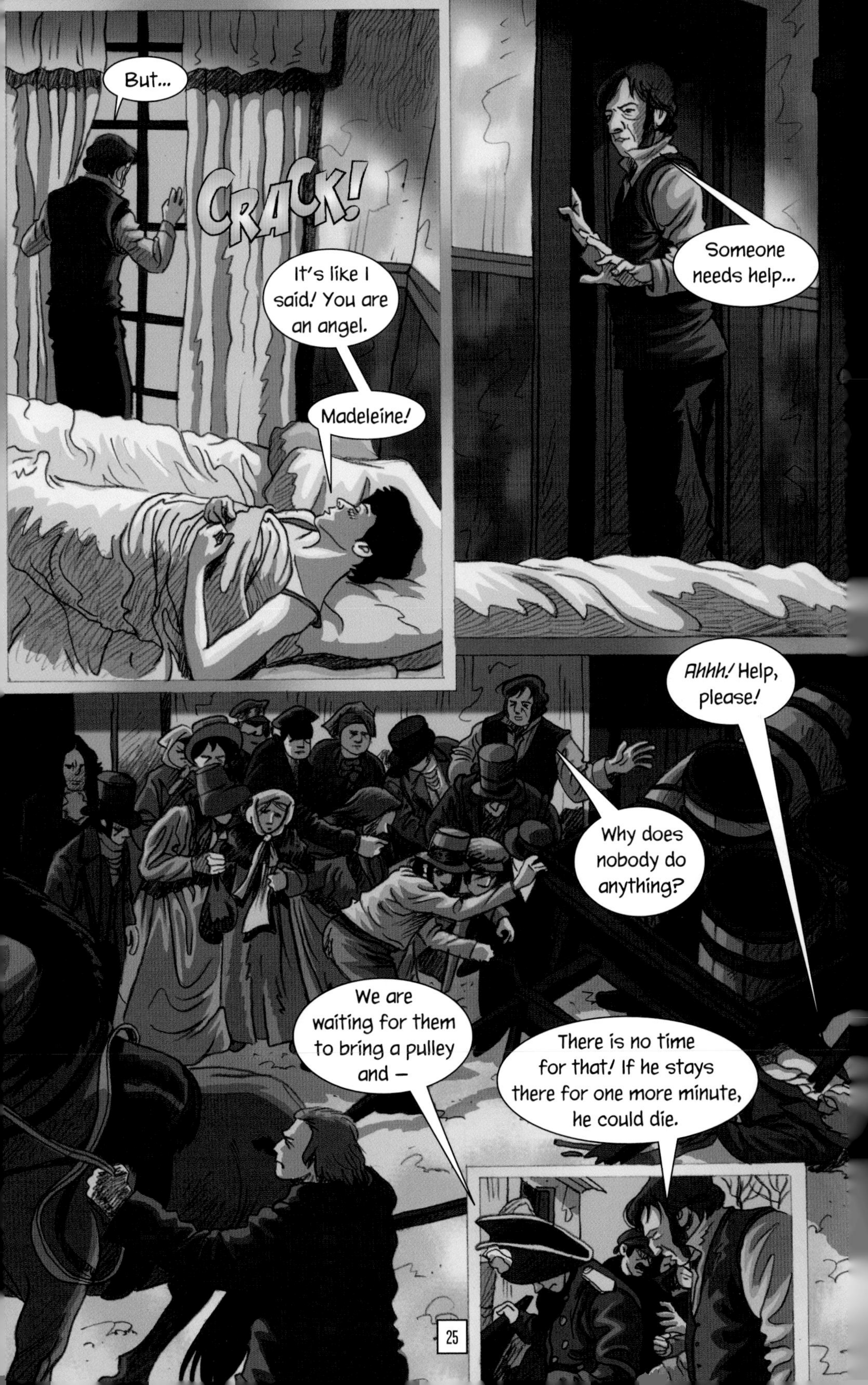
But...
CRACK!
It's like I said! You are an angel.
Madeleine!
Someone needs help...
Ahhh! Help, please!
Why does nobody do anything?
We are waiting for them to bring a pulley and –
There is no time for that! If he stays there for one more minute, he could die.

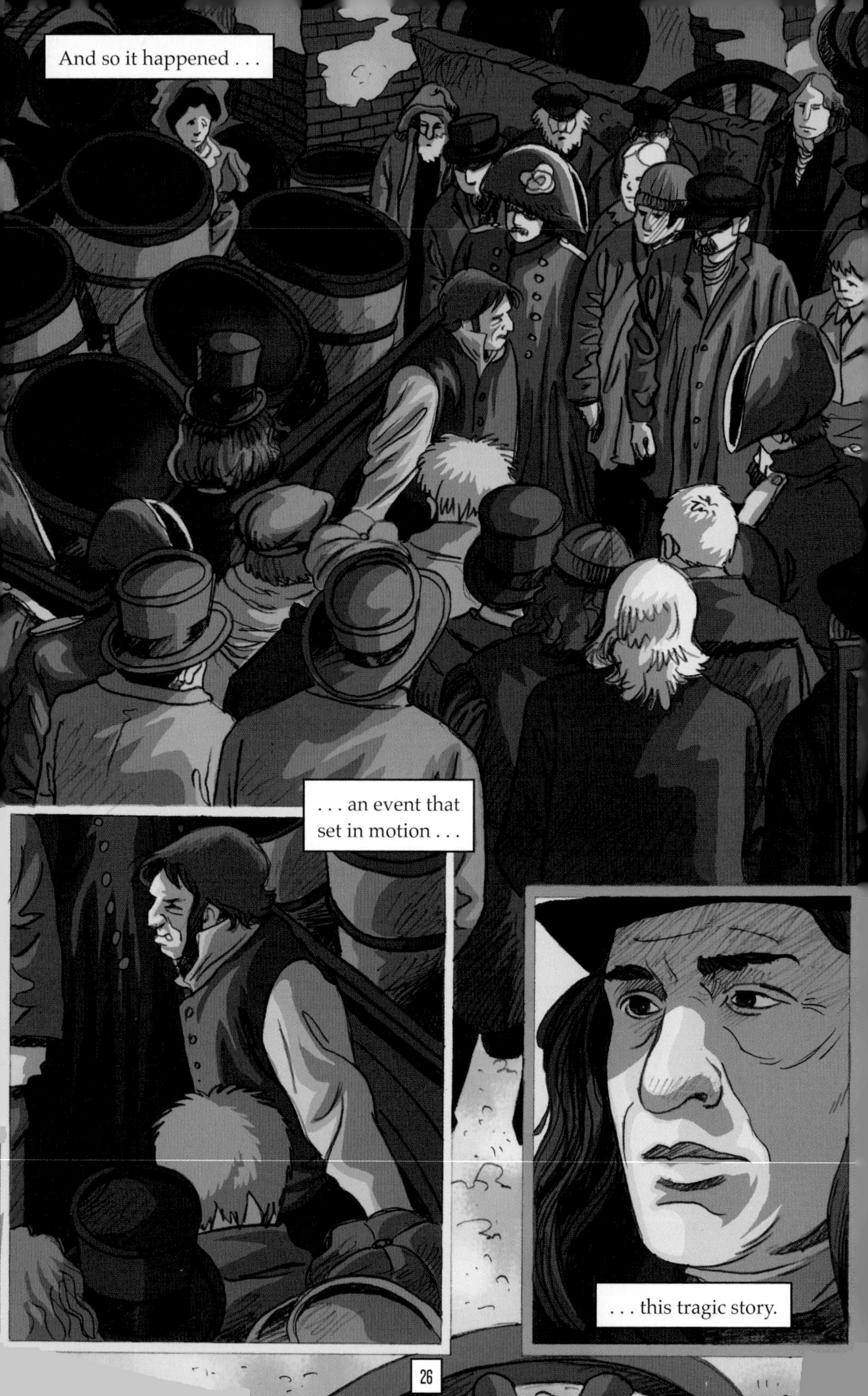
And so it happened . . .
. . . an event that set in motion . . .
. . . this tragic story.

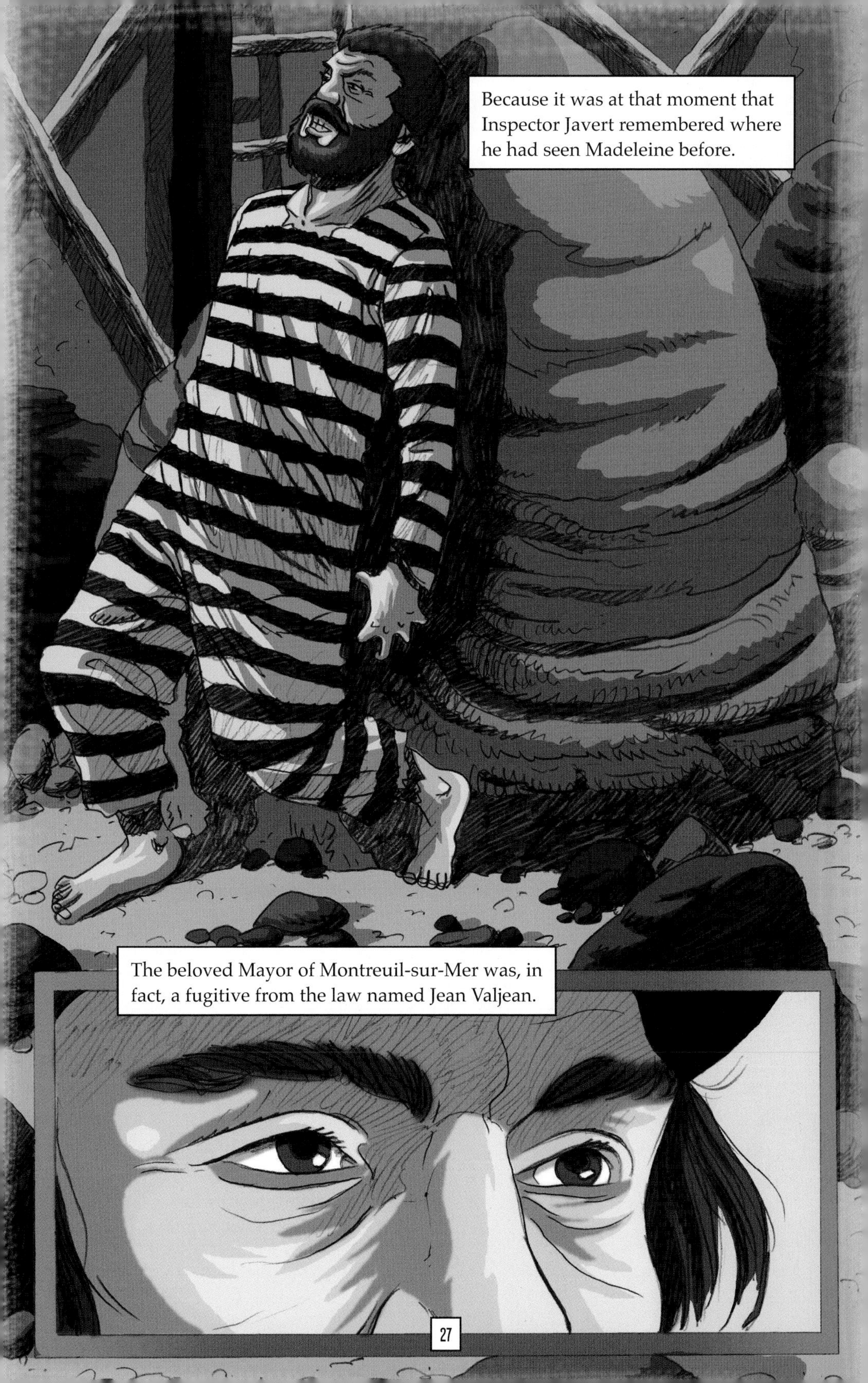
Because it was at that moment that Inspector Javert remembered where he had seen Madeleine before.
The beloved Mayor of Montreuil-sur-Mer was, in fact, a fugitive from the law named Jean Valjean.

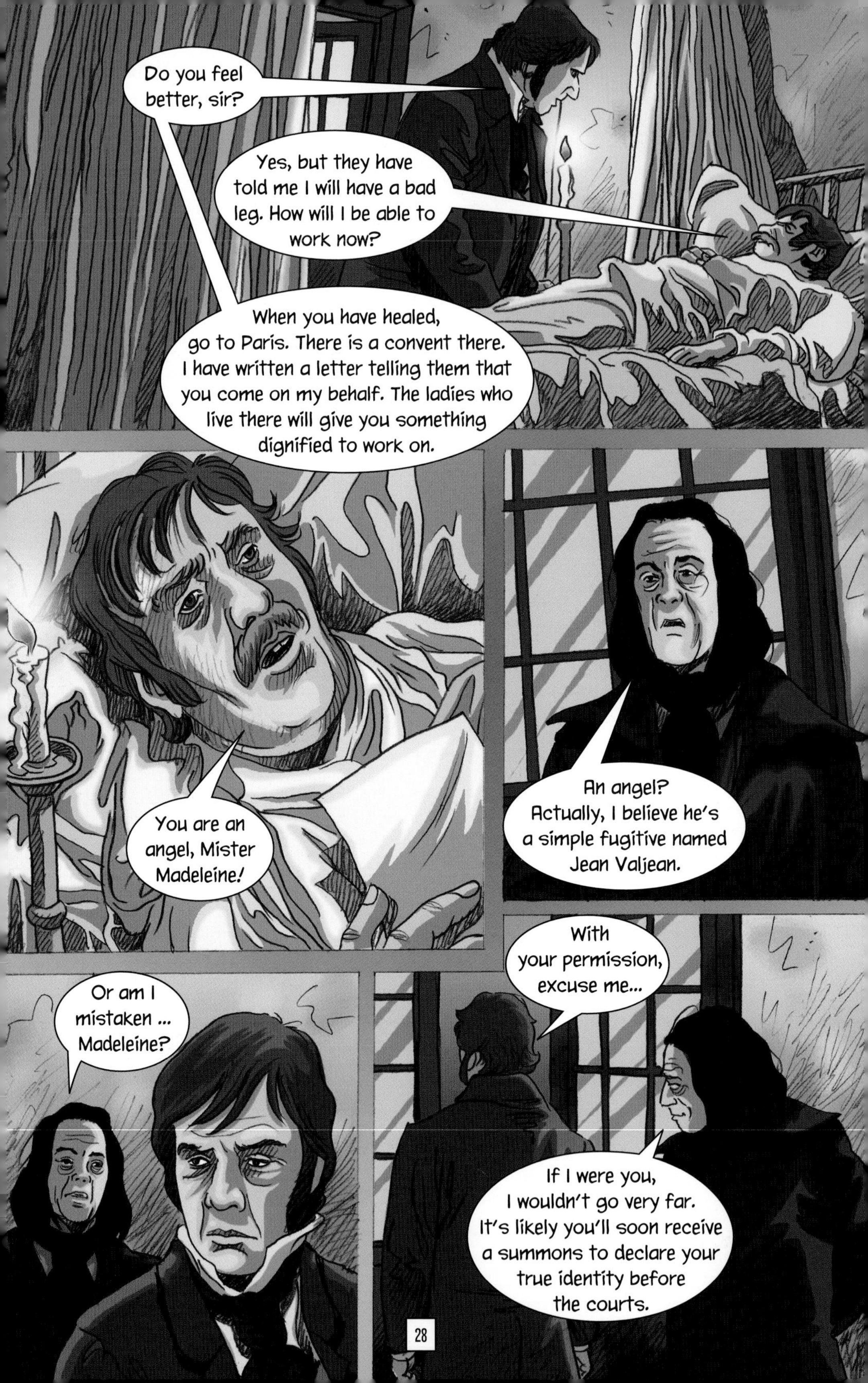
Do you feel better, sir?
Yes, but they have told me I will have a bad leg. How will I be able to work now?
When you have healed, go to Paris. There is a convent there. I have written a letter telling them that you come on my behalf. The ladies who live there will give you something dignified to work on.
You are an angel, Mister Madeleine!
An angel? Actually, I believe he's a simple fugitive named Jean Valjean.
Or am I mistaken ... Madeleine?
With your permission, excuse me...
If I were you, I wouldn't go very far. It's likely you'll soon receive a summons to declare your true identity before the courts.

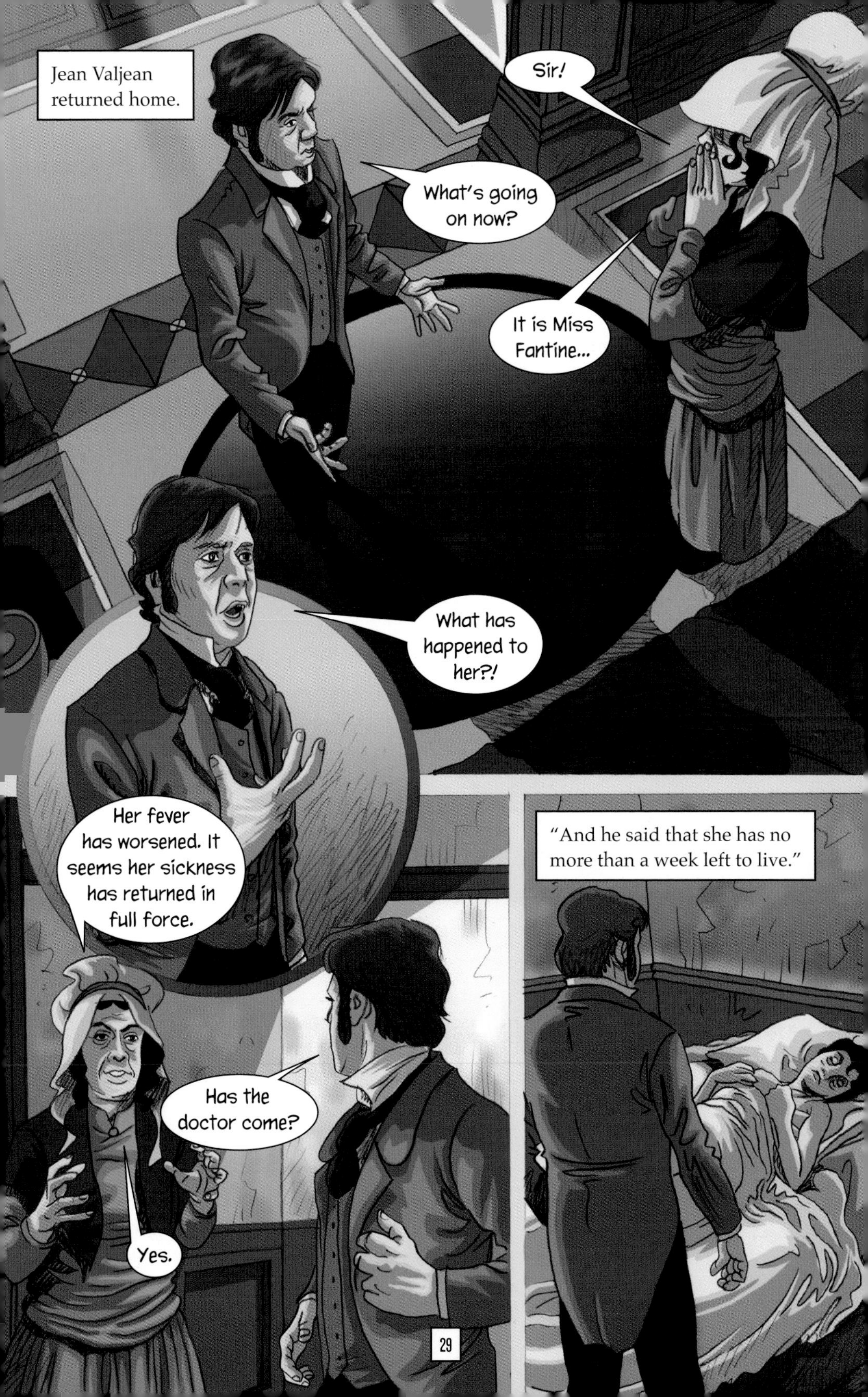

Jean Valjean returned home.
Sir!
What's going on now?
It is Miss Fantine...
What has happened to her?!
Her fever has worsened. It seems her sickness has returned in full force.
Has the doctor come?
Yes.
"And he said that she has no more than a week left to live."

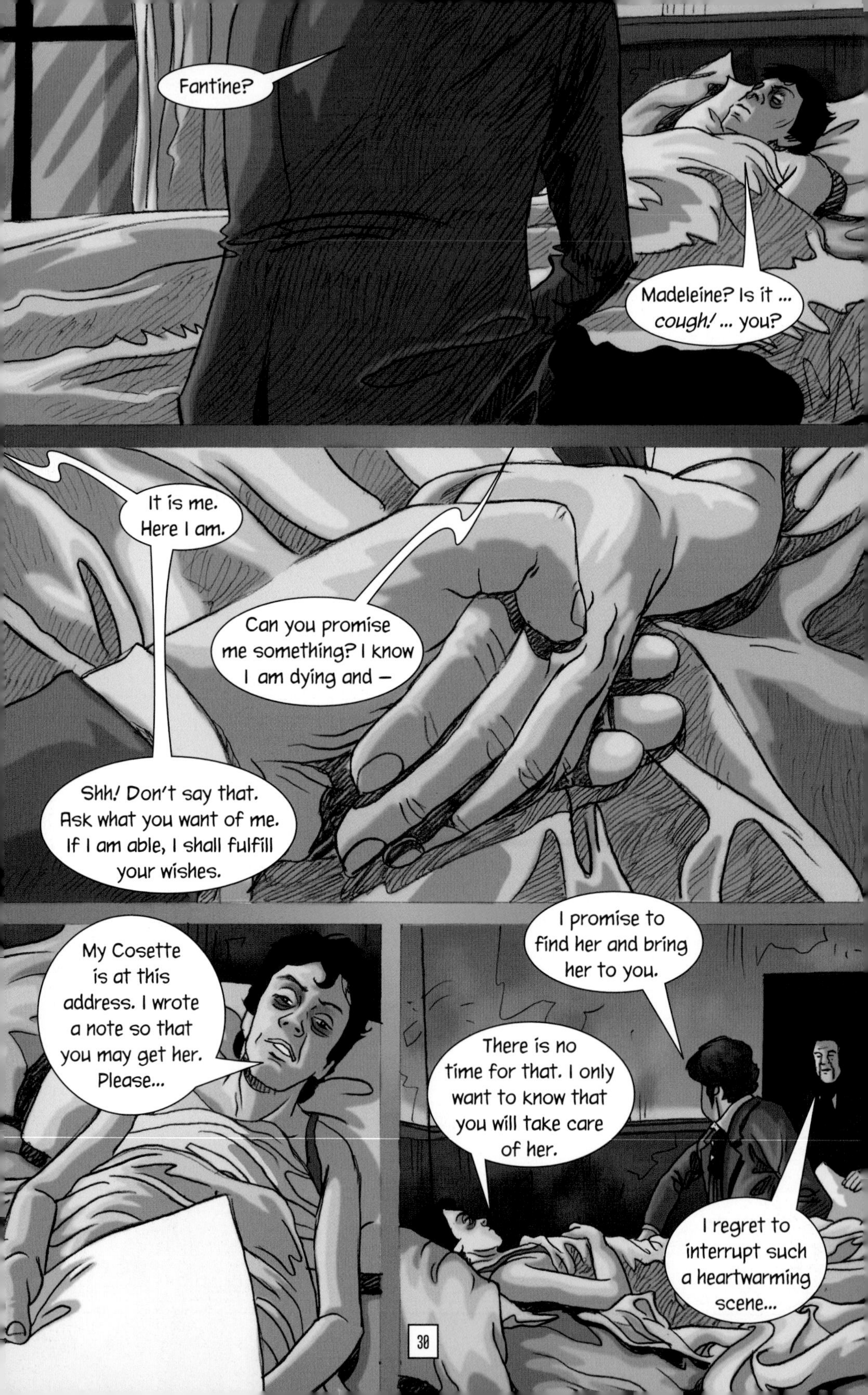
Fantine?
Madeleine? Is it ... *cough!* ... you?
It is me. Here I am.
Can you promise me something? I know I am dying and –
Shh! Don't say that. Ask what you want of me. If I am able, I shall fulfill your wishes.
My Cosette is at this address. I wrote a note so that you may get her. Please...
I promise to find her and bring her to you.
There is no time for that. I only want to know that you will take care of her.
I regret to interrupt such a heartwarming scene...

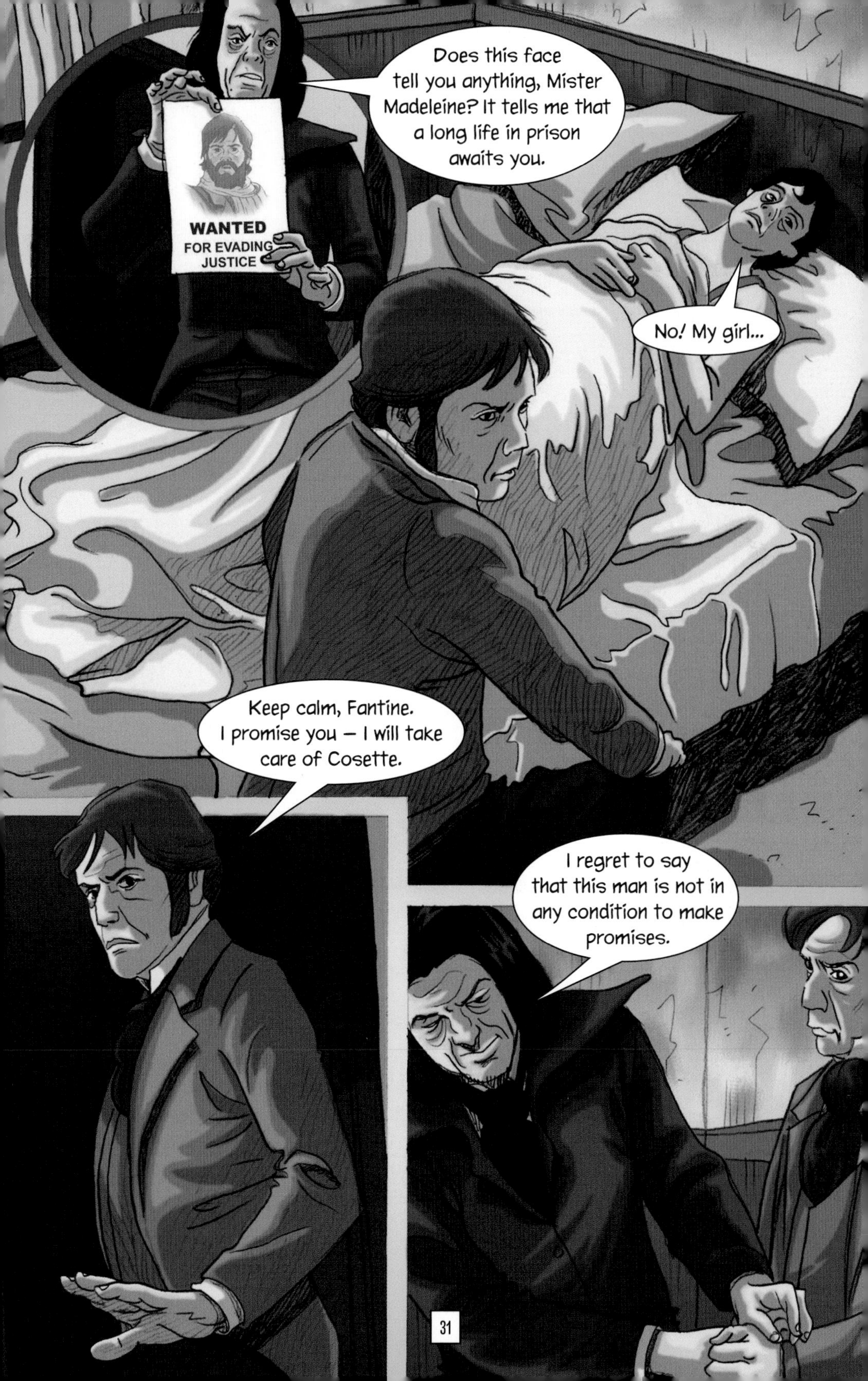
WANTED
FOR EVADING JUSTICE
Does this face tell you anything, Mister Madeleine? It tells me that a long life in prison awaits you.
No! My girl...
Keep calm, Fantine. I promise you — I will take care of Cosette.
I regret to say that this man is not in any condition to make promises.

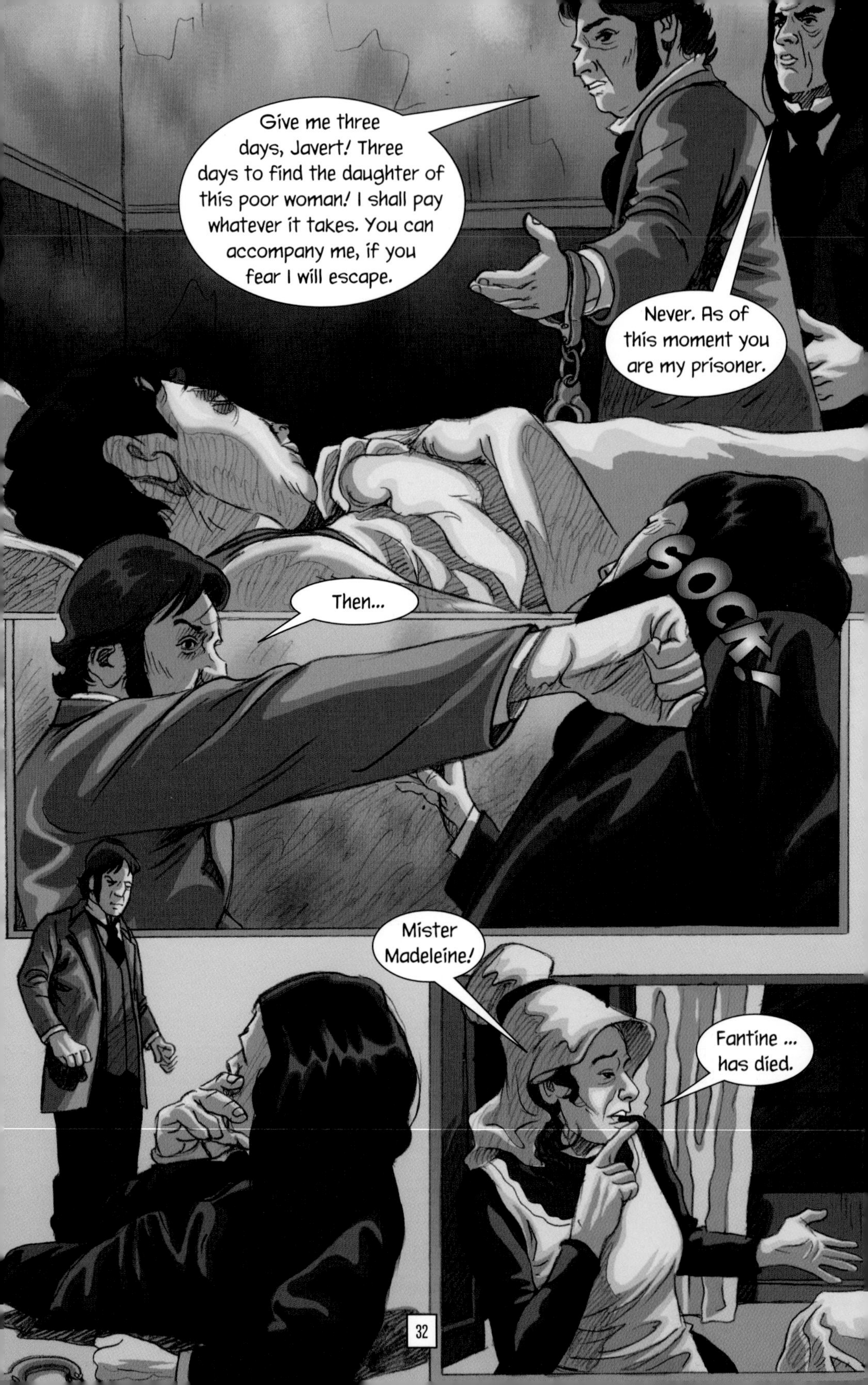

Give me three days, Javert! Three days to find the daughter of this poor woman! I shall pay whatever it takes. You can accompany me, if you fear I will escape.
Never. As of this moment you are my prisoner.
Then...
SOCK!
Mister Madeleine!
Fantine ... has died.

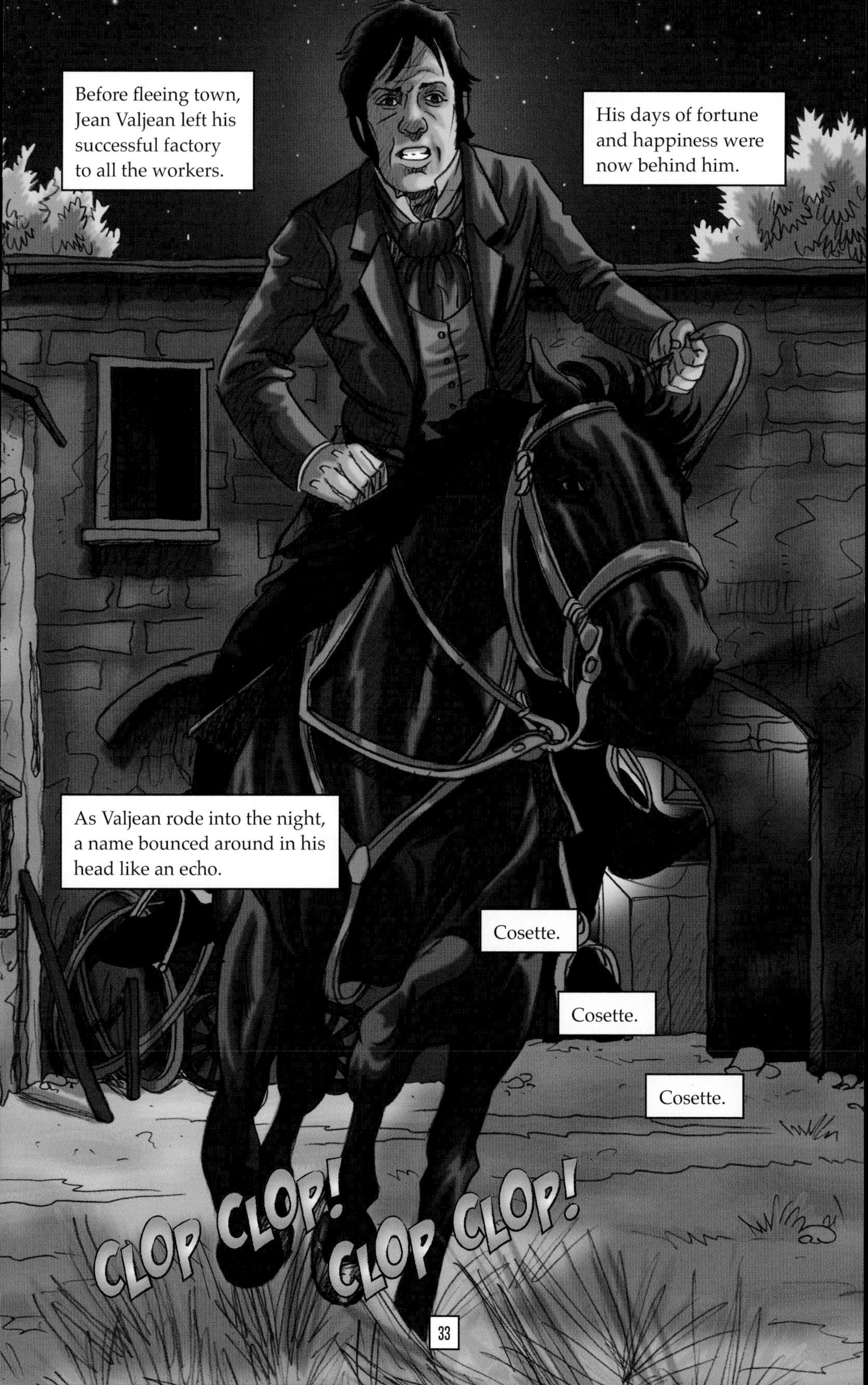
Before fleeing town, Jean Valjean left his successful factory to all the workers.
His days of fortune and happiness were now behind him.
As Valjean rode into the night, a name bounced around in his head like an echo.
Cosette.
Cosette.
Cosette.
CLOP CLOP!
CLOP CLOP!

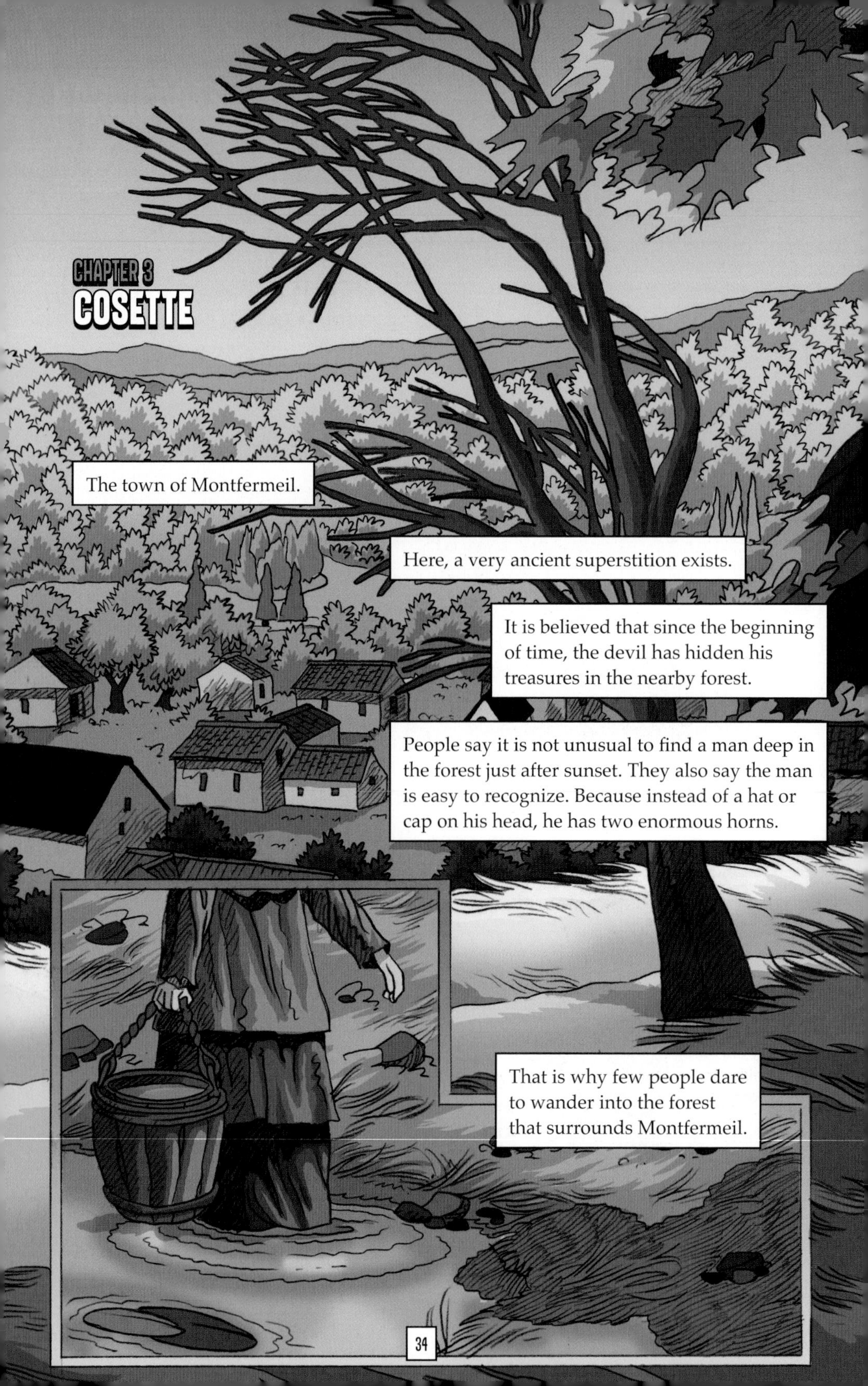
CHAPTER 3
COSETTE
The town of Montfermeil.
Here, a very ancient superstition exists.
It is believed that since the beginning of time, the devil has hidden his treasures in the nearby forest.
People say it is not unusual to find a man deep in the forest just after sunset. They also say the man is easy to recognize. Because instead of a hat or cap on his head, he has two enormous horns.
That is why few people dare to wander into the forest that surrounds Montfermeil.

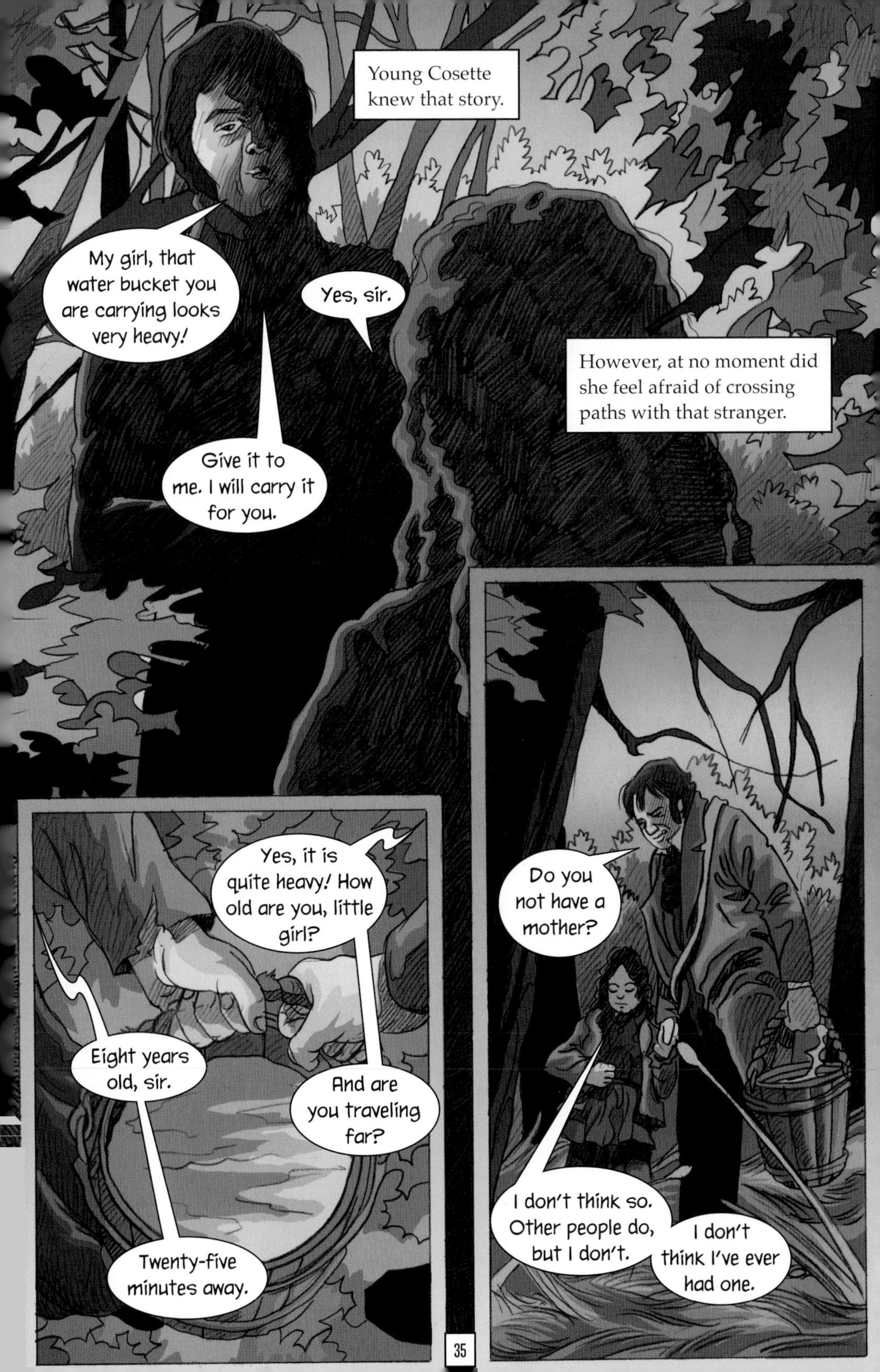
Young Cosette knew that story.
My girl, that water bucket you are carrying looks very heavy!
Yes, sir.
Give it to me. I will carry it for you.
However, at no moment did she feel afraid of crossing paths with that stranger.
Yes, it is quite heavy! How old are you, little girl?
Eight years old, sir.
And are you traveling far?
Twenty-five minutes away.
Do you not have a mother?
I don't think so. Other people do, but I don't.
I don't think I've ever had one.

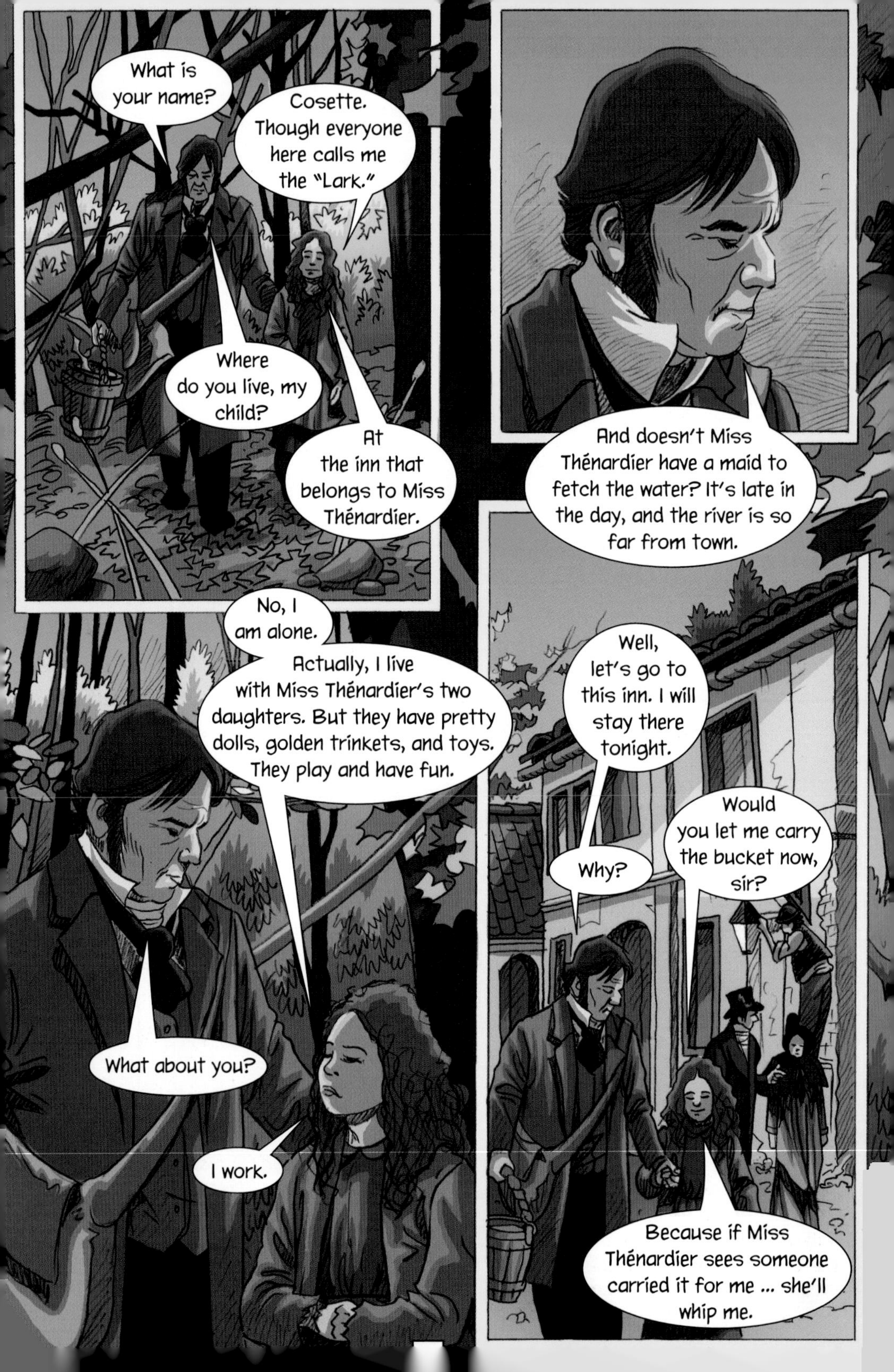

What is your name?
Cosette. Though everyone here calls me the "Lark."
Where do you live, my child?
At the inn that belongs to Miss Thénardier.
And doesn't Miss Thénardier have a maid to fetch the water? It's late in the day, and the river is so far from town.
No, I am alone.
Actually, I live with Miss Thénardier's two daughters. But they have pretty dolls, golden trinkets, and toys. They play and have fun.
What about you?
I work.
Well, let's go to this inn. I will stay there tonight.
Would you let me carry the bucket now, sir?
Why?
Because if Miss Thénardier sees someone carried it for me ... she'll whip me.

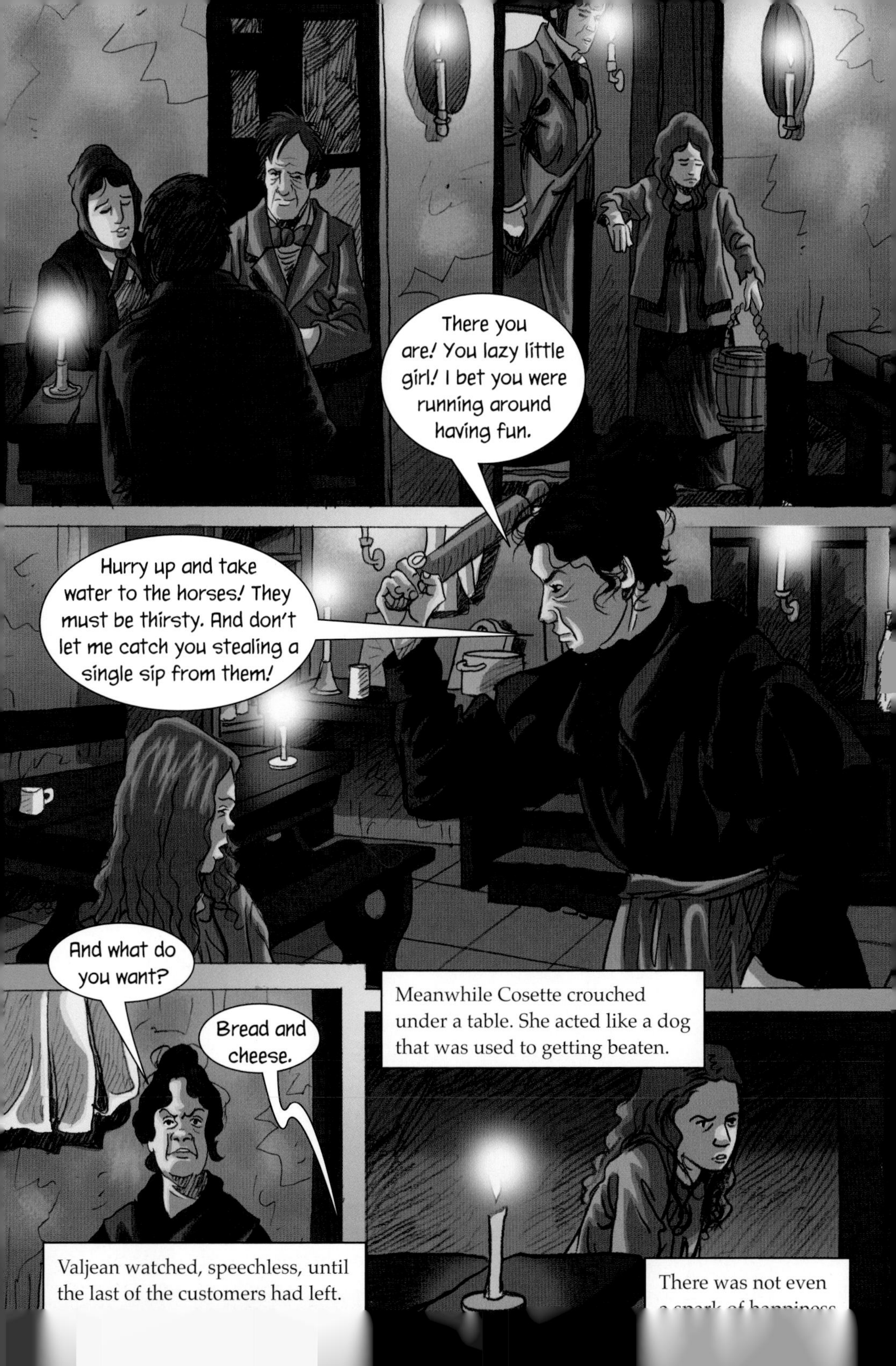

There you are! You lazy little girl! I bet you were running around having fun.
Hurry up and take water to the horses! They must be thirsty. And don't let me catch you stealing a single sip from them!
And what do you want?
Bread and cheese.
Valjean watched, speechless, until the last of the customers had left.
Meanwhile Cosette crouched under a table. She acted like a dog that was used to getting beaten.
There was not even

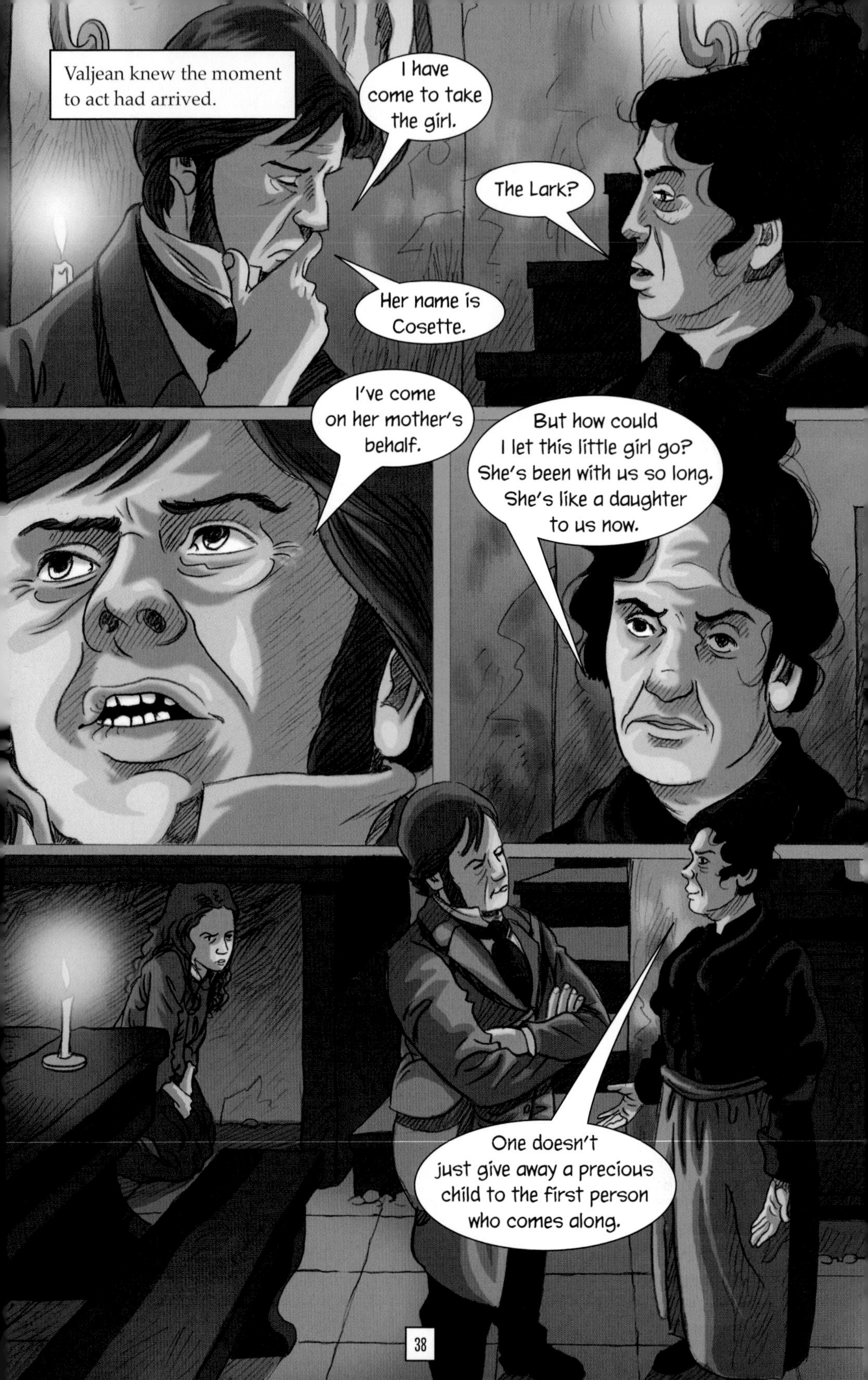
Valjean knew the moment to act had arrived.
I have come to take the girl.
The Lark?
Her name is Cosette.
I've come on her mother's behalf.
But how could I let this little girl go? She's been with us so long. She's like a daughter to us now.
One doesn't just give away a precious child to the first person who comes along.

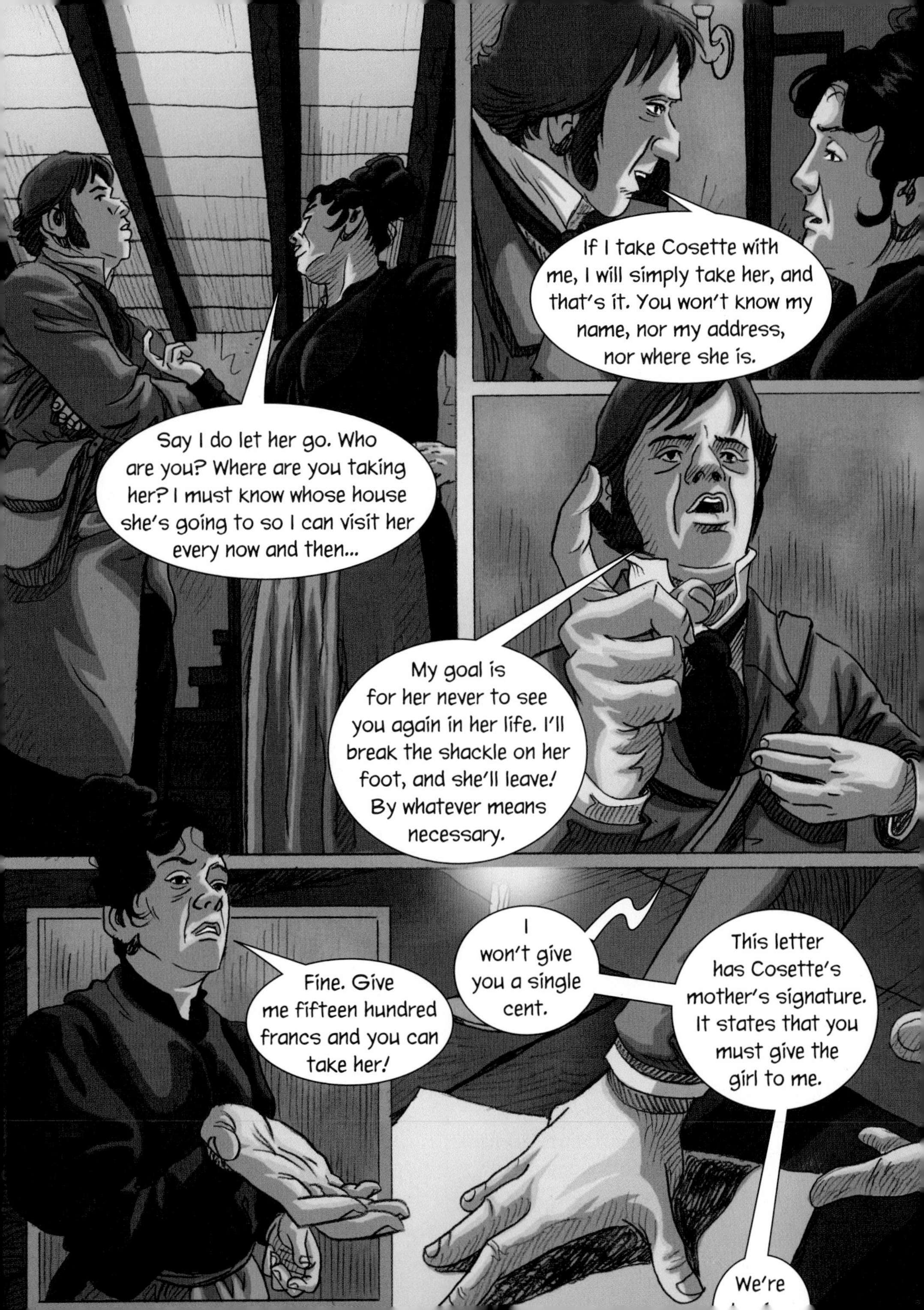
Say I do let her go. Who are you? Where are you taking her? I must know whose house she's going to so I can visit her every now and then...
If I take Cosette with me, I will simply take her, and that's it. You won't know my name, nor my address, nor where she is.
My goal is for her never to see you again in her life. I'll break the shackle on her foot, and she'll leave! By whatever means necessary.
Fine. Give me fifteen hundred francs and you can take her!
I won't give you a single cent.
This letter has Cosette's mother's signature. It states that you must give the girl to me.
We're

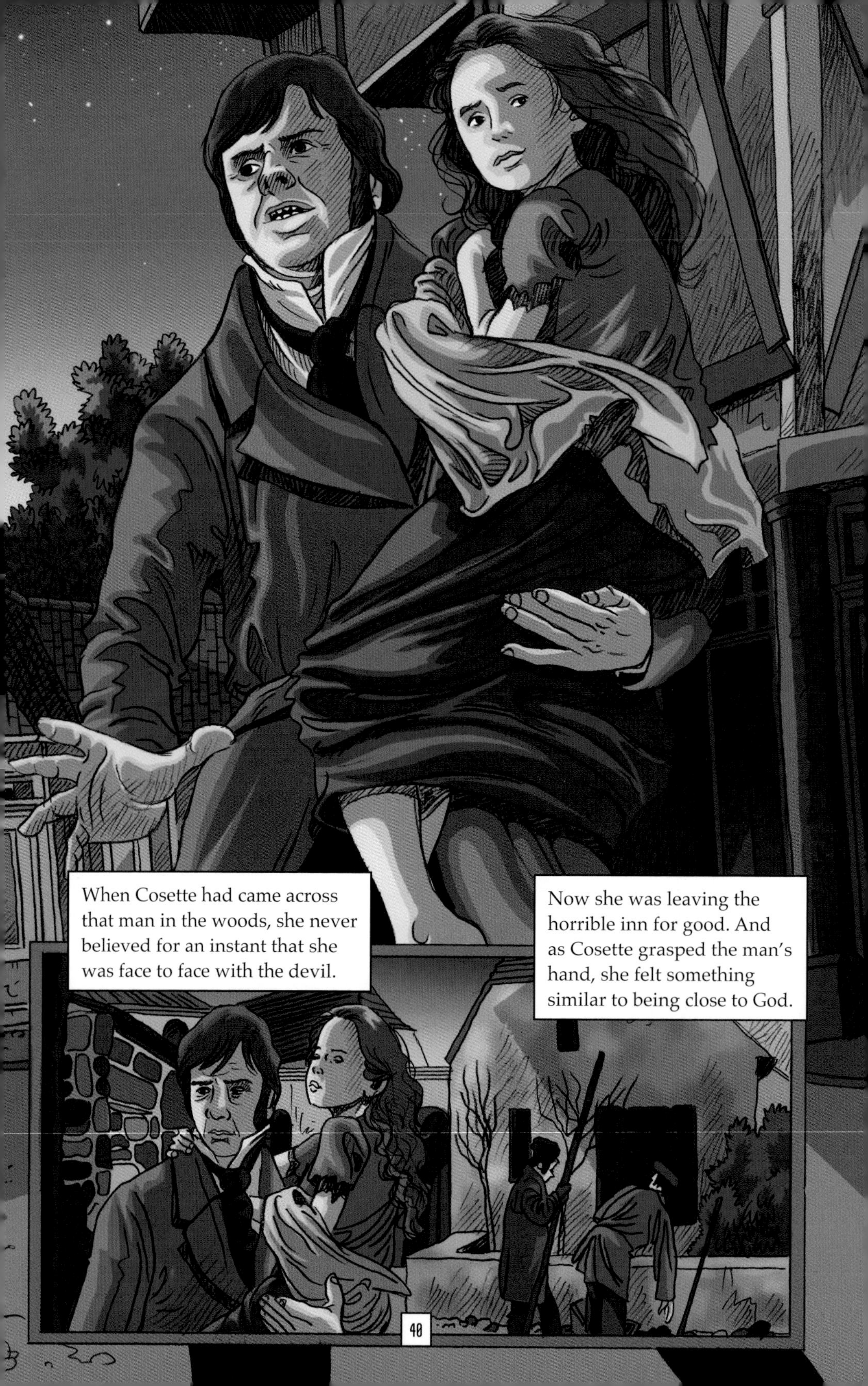
When Cosette had came across that man in the woods, she never believed for an instant that she was face to face with the devil.
Now she was leaving the horrible inn for good. And as Cosette grasped the man's hand, she felt something similar to being close to God.

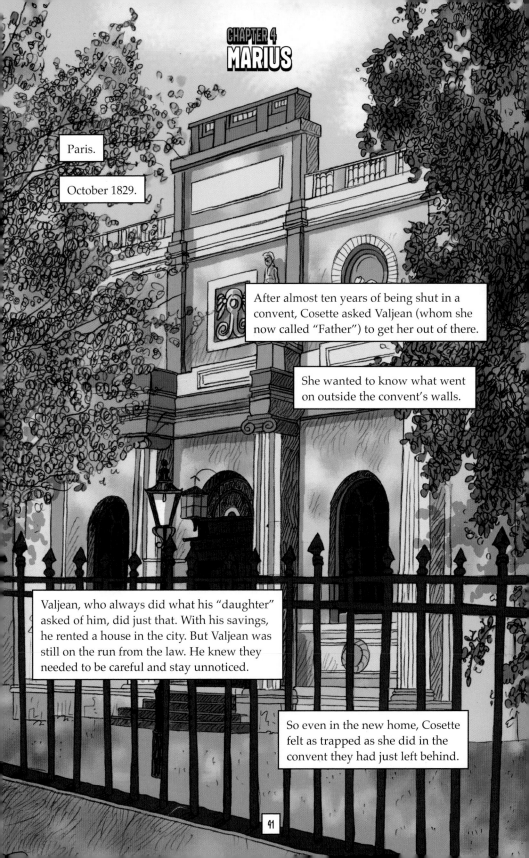

Paris.

October 1829.

After almost ten years of being shut in a convent, Cosette asked Valjean (whom she now called "Father") to get her out of there.

She wanted to know what went on outside the convent's walls.

Valjean, who always did what his "daughter" asked of him, did just that. With his savings, he rented a house in the city. But Valjean was still on the run from the law. He knew they needed to be careful and stay unnoticed.

So even in the new home, Cosette felt as trapped as she did in the convent they had just left behind.

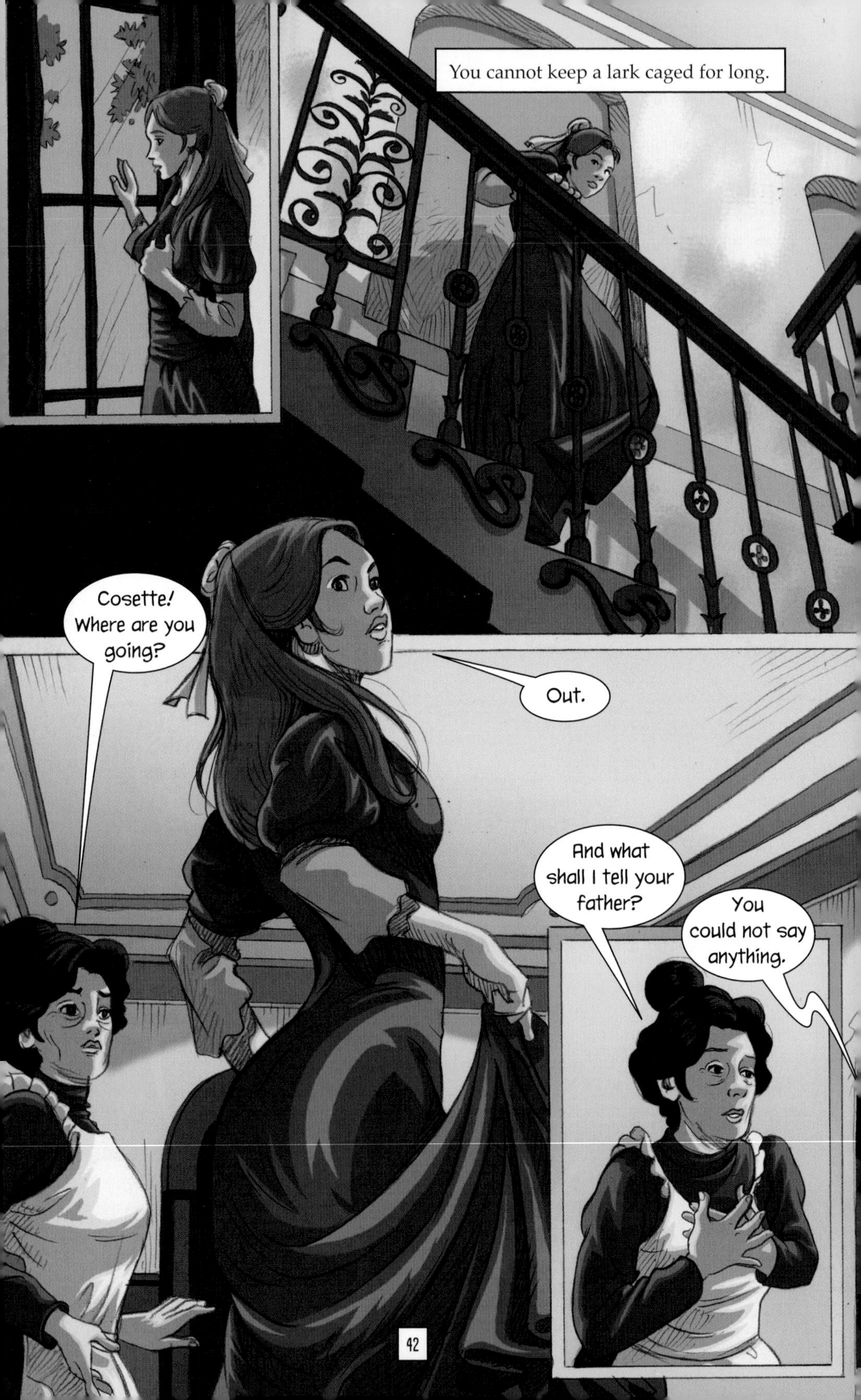
You cannot keep a lark caged for long.
Cosette! Where are you going?
Out.
And what shall I tell your father?
You could not say anything.

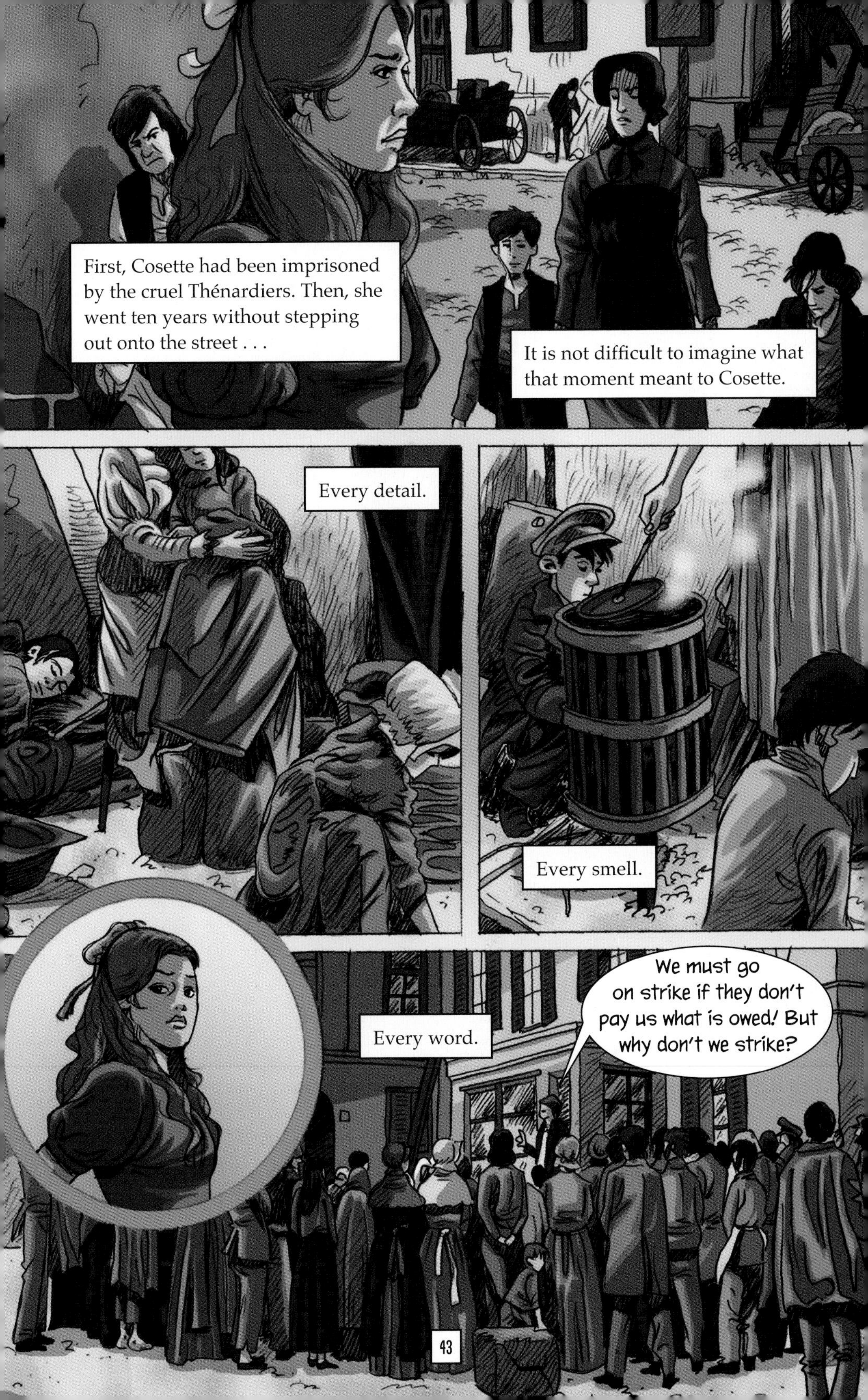

First, Cosette had been imprisoned by the cruel Thénardiers. Then, she went ten years without stepping out onto the street . . .
It is not difficult to imagine what that moment meant to Cosette.
Every detail.
Every smell.
Every word.
We must go on strike if they don't pay us what is owed! But why don't we strike?

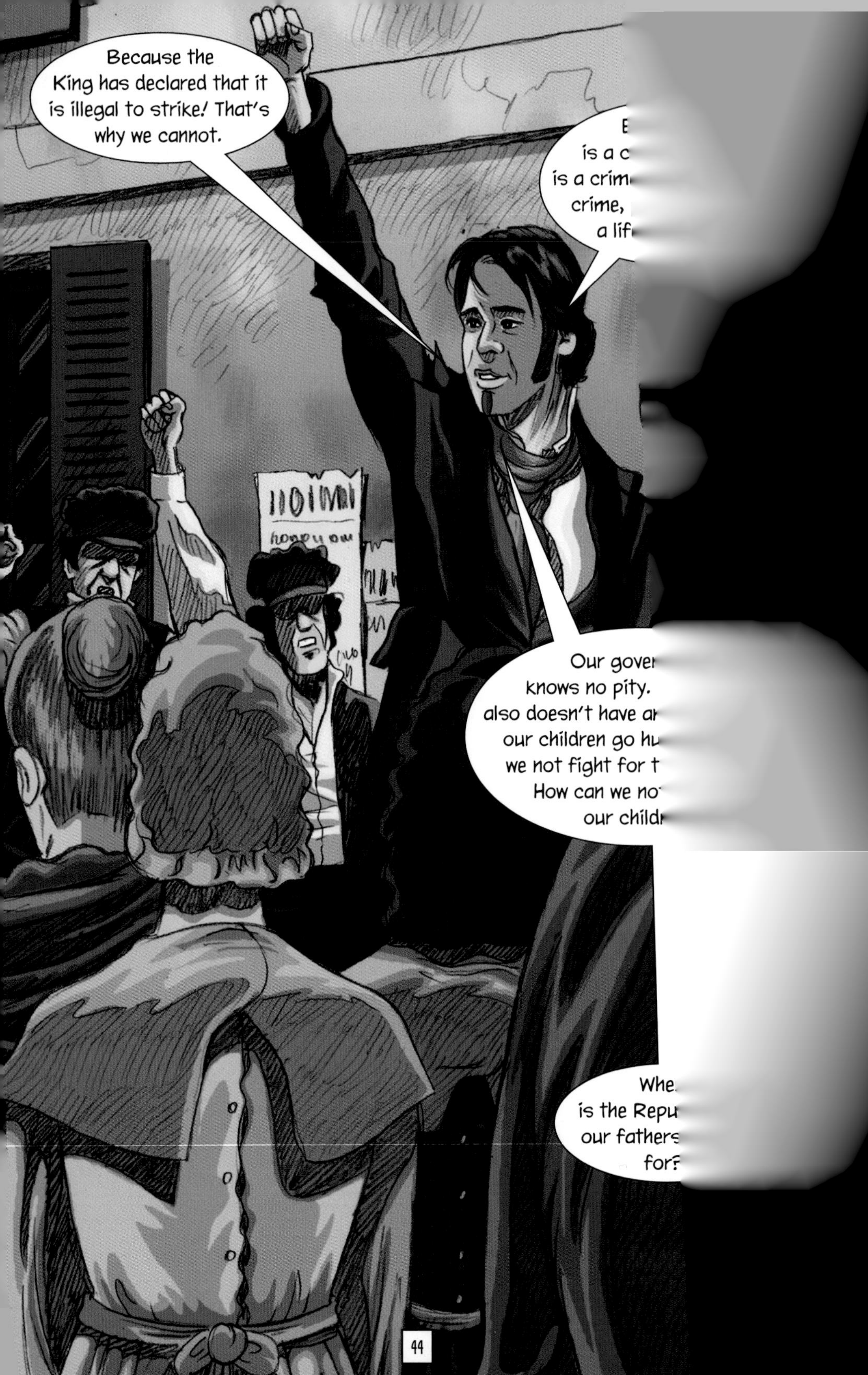
Because the King has declared that it is illegal to strike! That's why we cannot.
crime,
knows no pity.
our children go
we not fight for
How can we
is the
for?

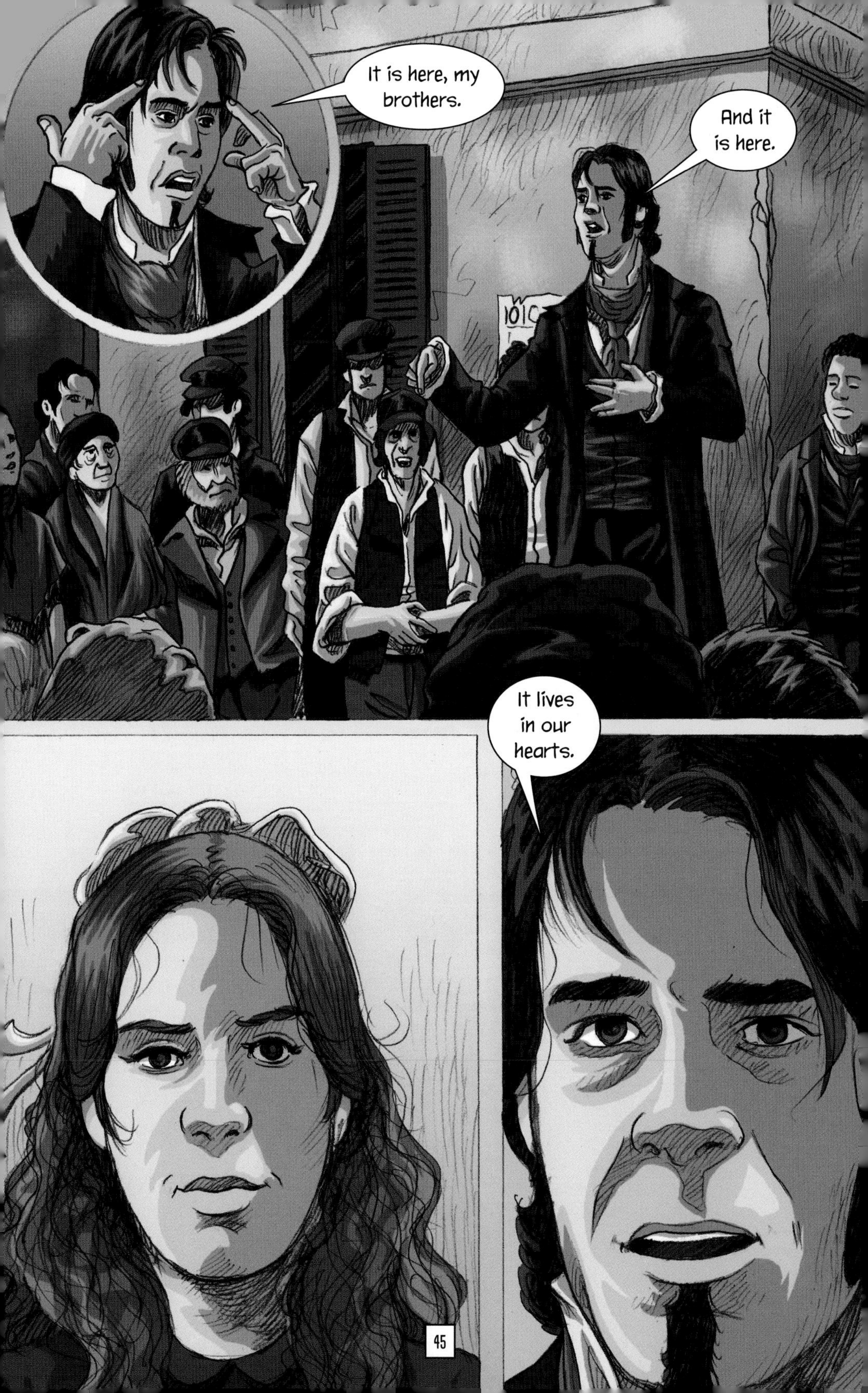
It is here, my brothers.
And it is here.
It lives in our hearts.

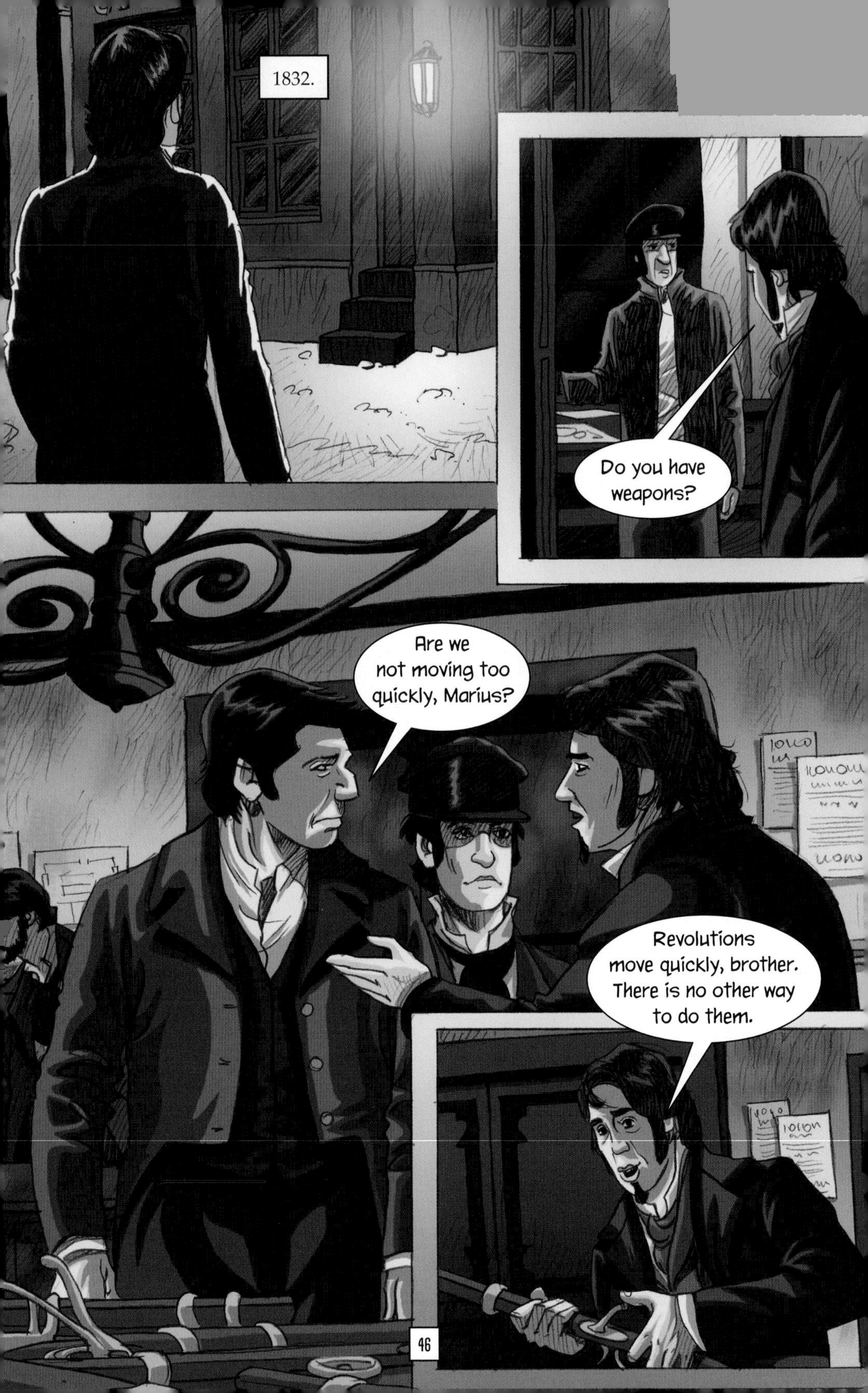
1832.
Do you have weapons?
Are we not moving too quickly, Marius?
Revolutions move quickly, brother. There is no other way to do them.

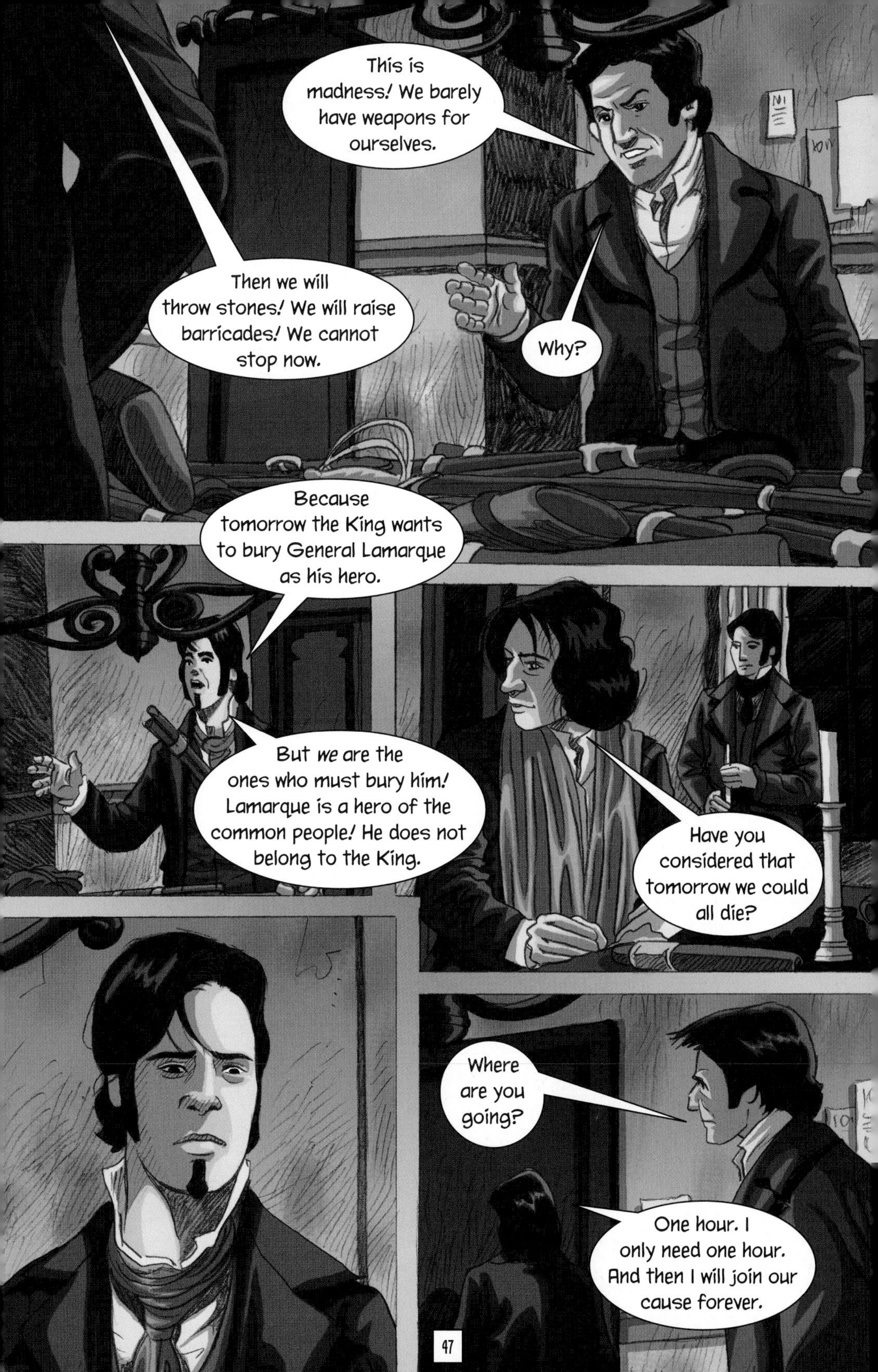

This is madness! We barely have weapons for ourselves.
Then we will throw stones! We will raise barricades! We cannot stop now.
Why?
Because tomorrow the King wants to bury General Lamarque as his hero.
But *we* are the ones who must bury him! Lamarque is a hero of the common people! He does not belong to the King.
Have you considered that tomorrow we could all die?
Where are you going?
One hour. I only need one hour. And then I will join our cause forever.

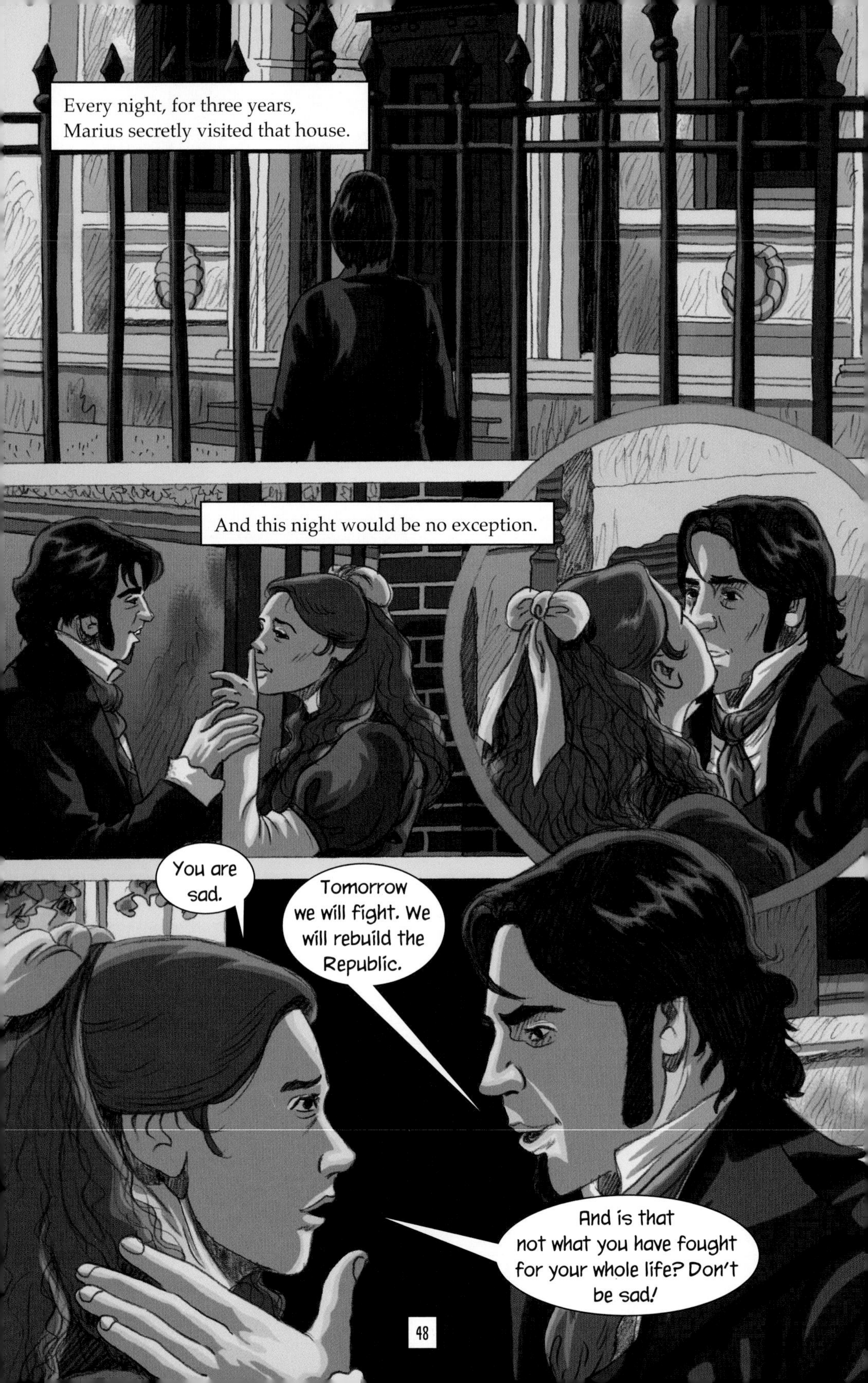
Every night, for three years,
Marius secretly visited that house.
And this night would be no exception.
You are sad.
Tomorrow we will fight. We will rebuild the Republic.
And is that not what you have fought for your whole life? Don't be sad!

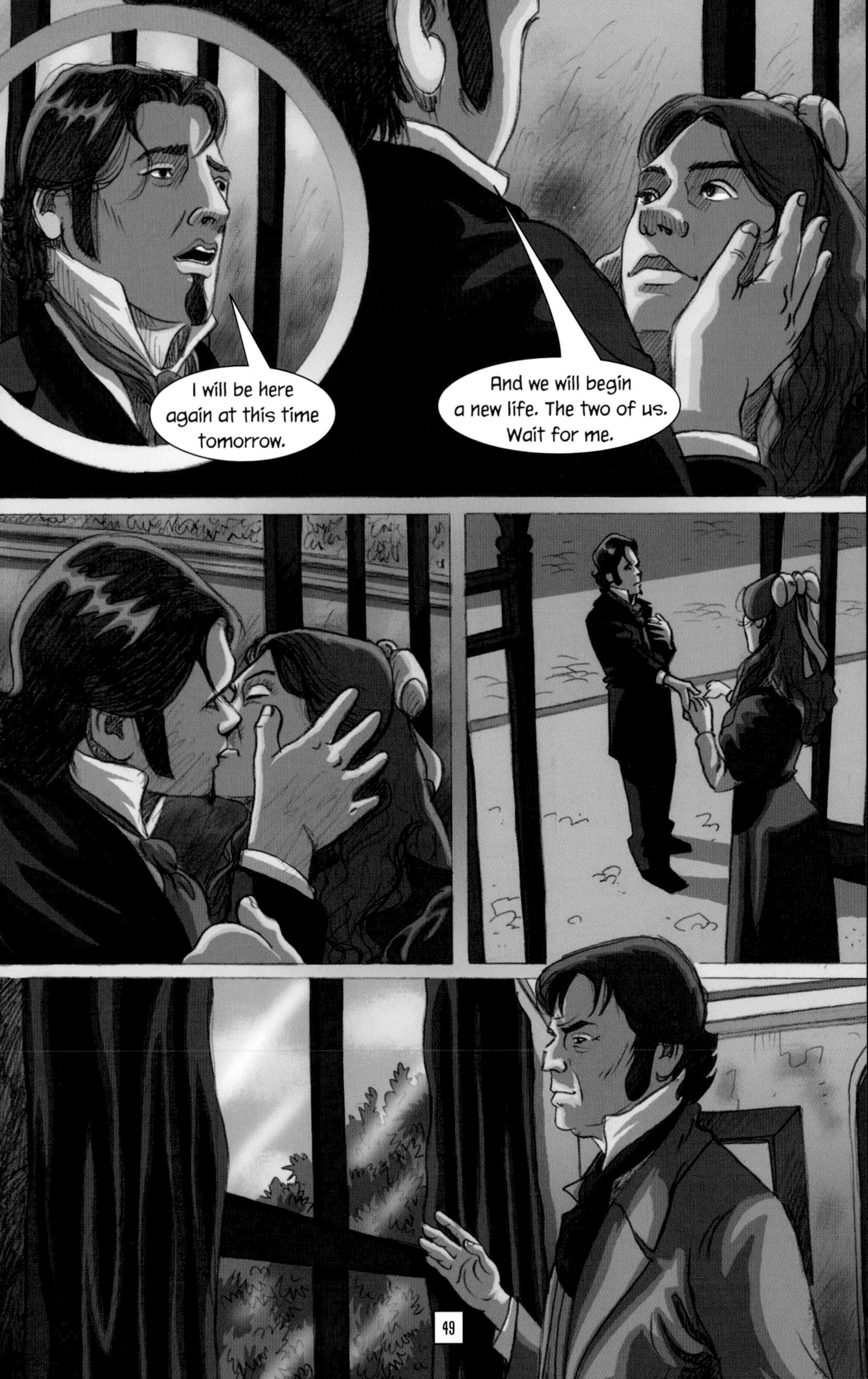
I will be here again at this time tomorrow.
And we will begin a new life. The two of us. Wait for me.

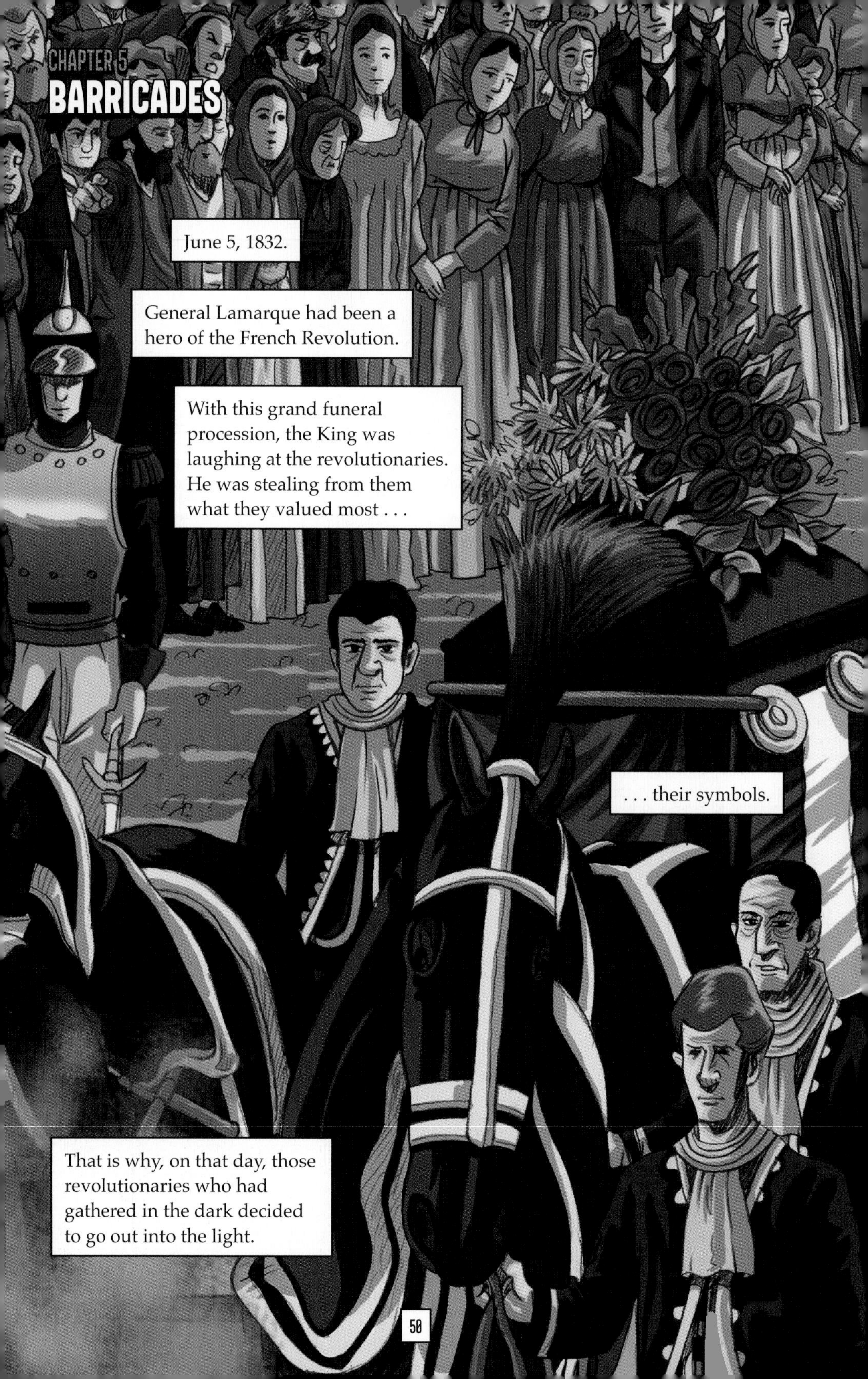
CHAPTER 5
BARRICADES
June 5, 1832.
General Lamarque had been a hero of the French Revolution.
With this grand funeral procession, the King was laughing at the revolutionaries. He was stealing from them what they valued most . . .
. . . their symbols.
That is why, on that day, those revolutionaries who had gathered in the dark decided to go out into the light.

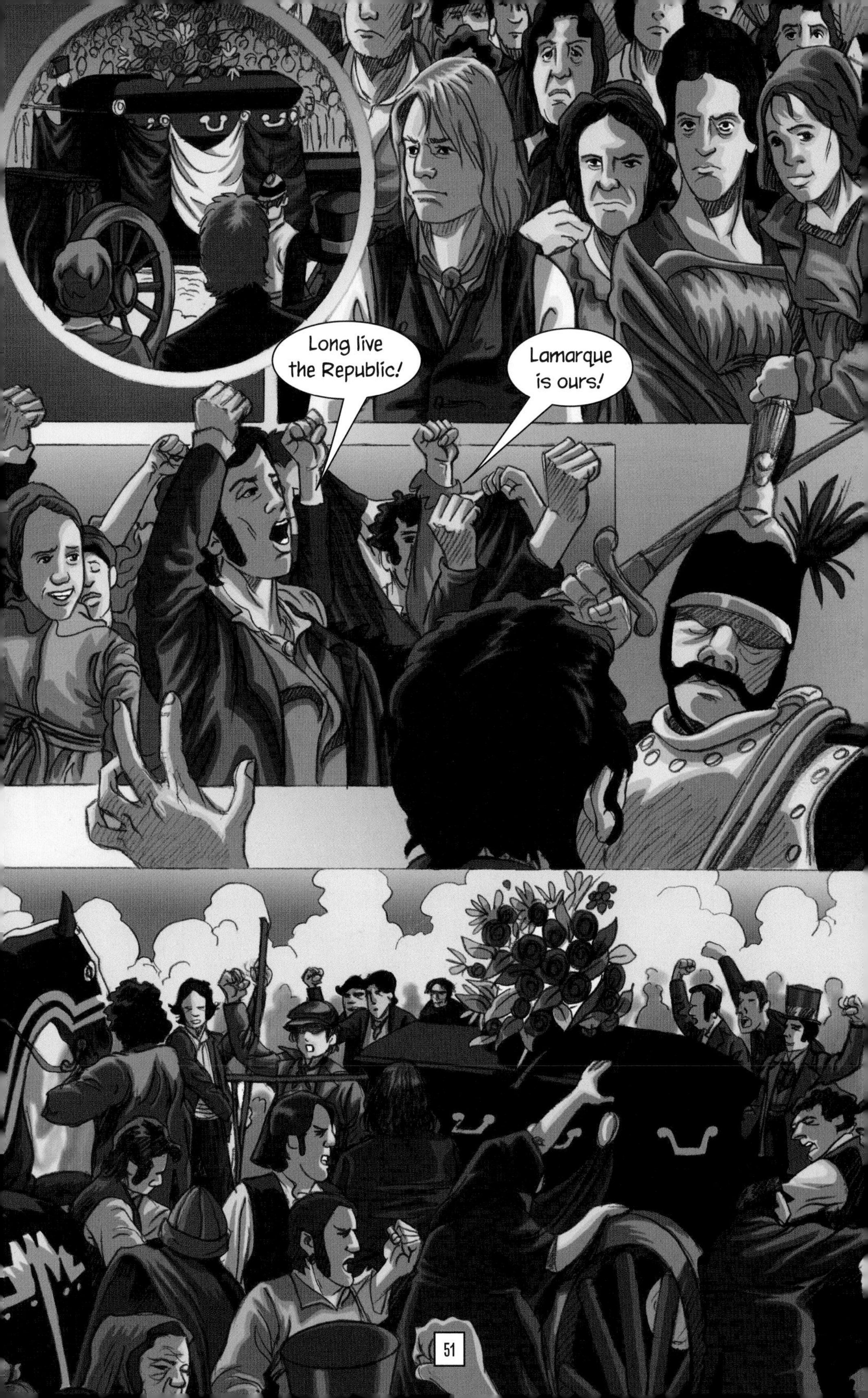
Long live the Republic!
Lamarque is ours!

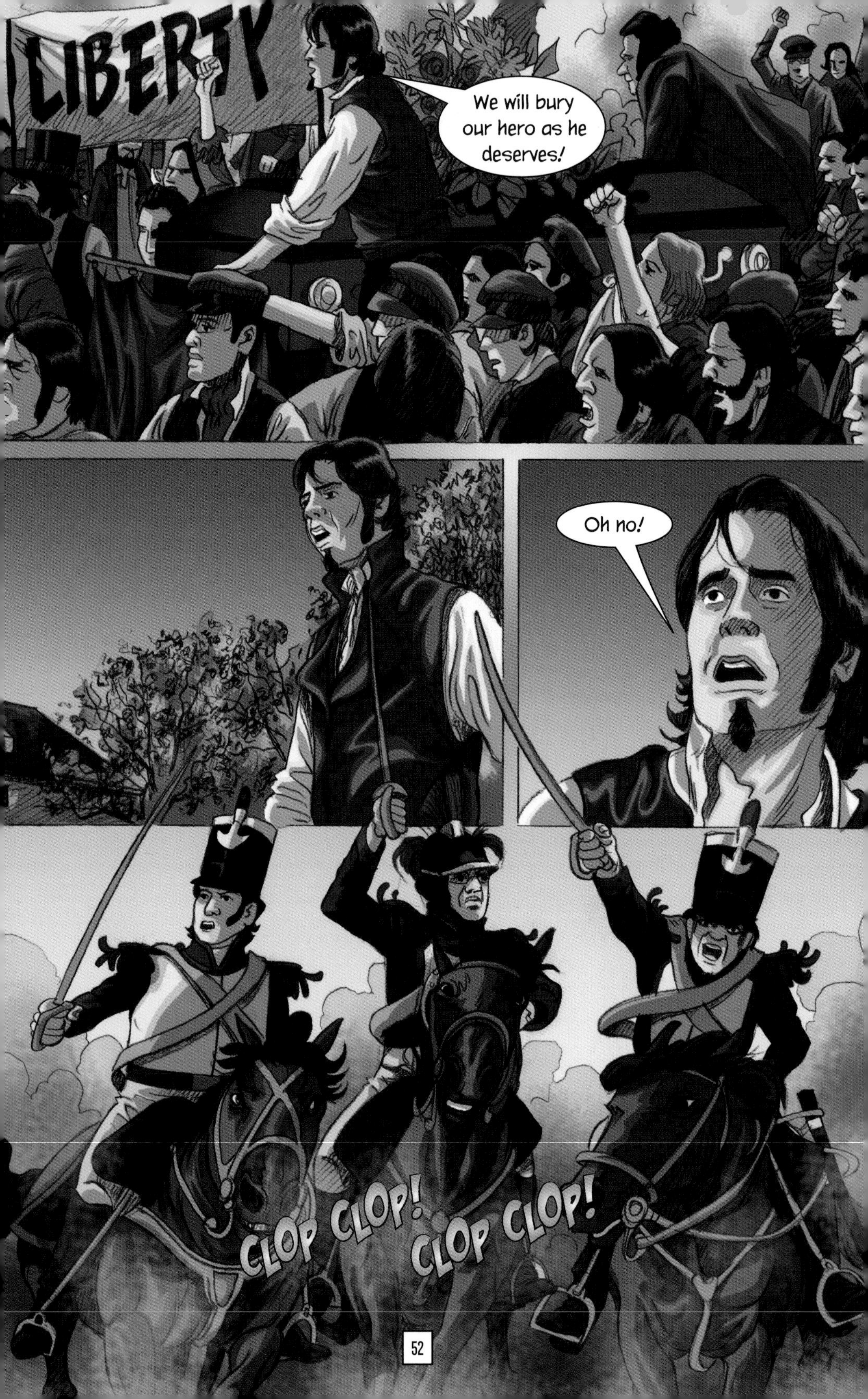
LIBERTY
We will bury our hero as he deserves!
Oh no!
CLOP CLOP!
CLOP CLOP!

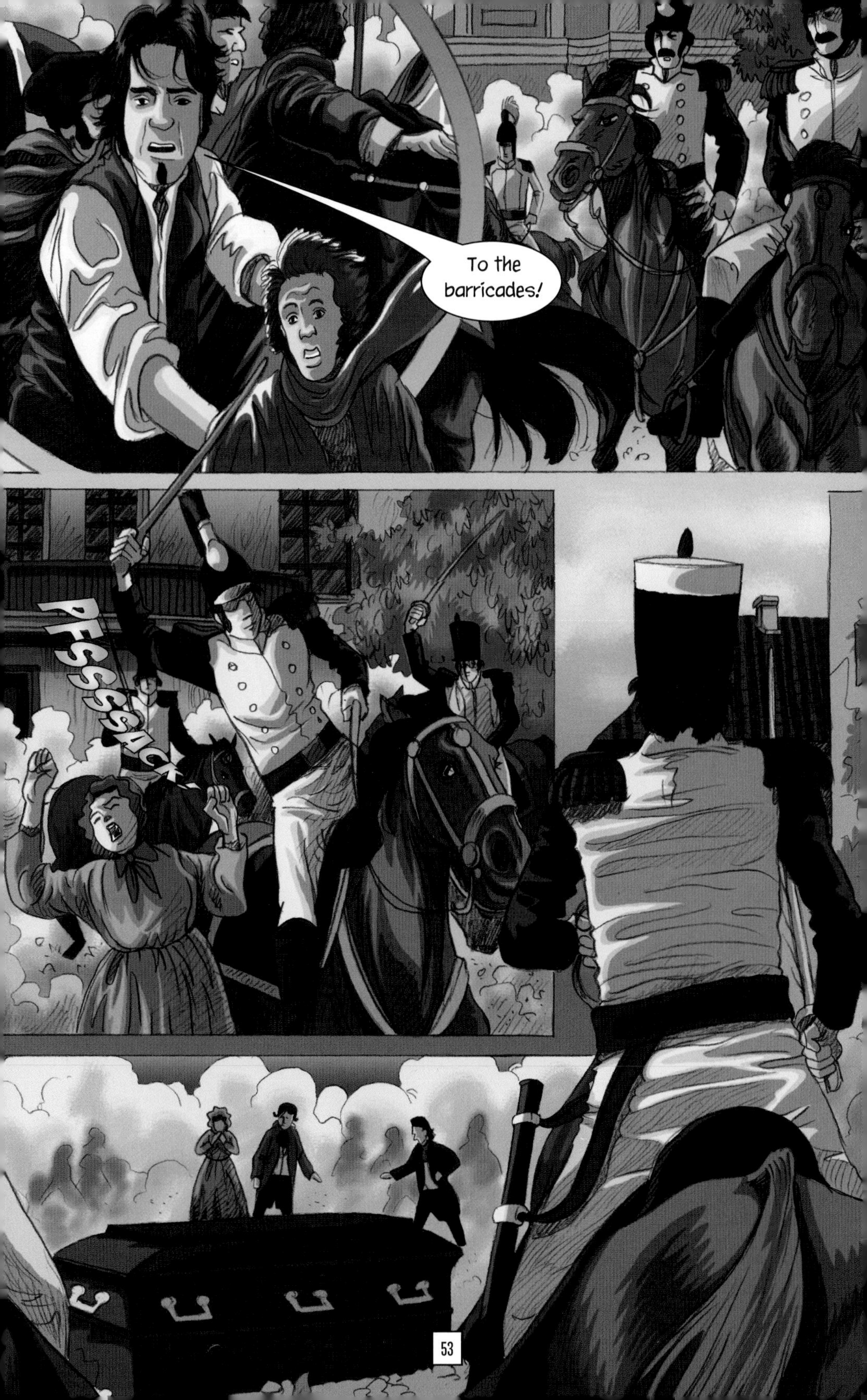
To the barricades!
PFSSSACK!

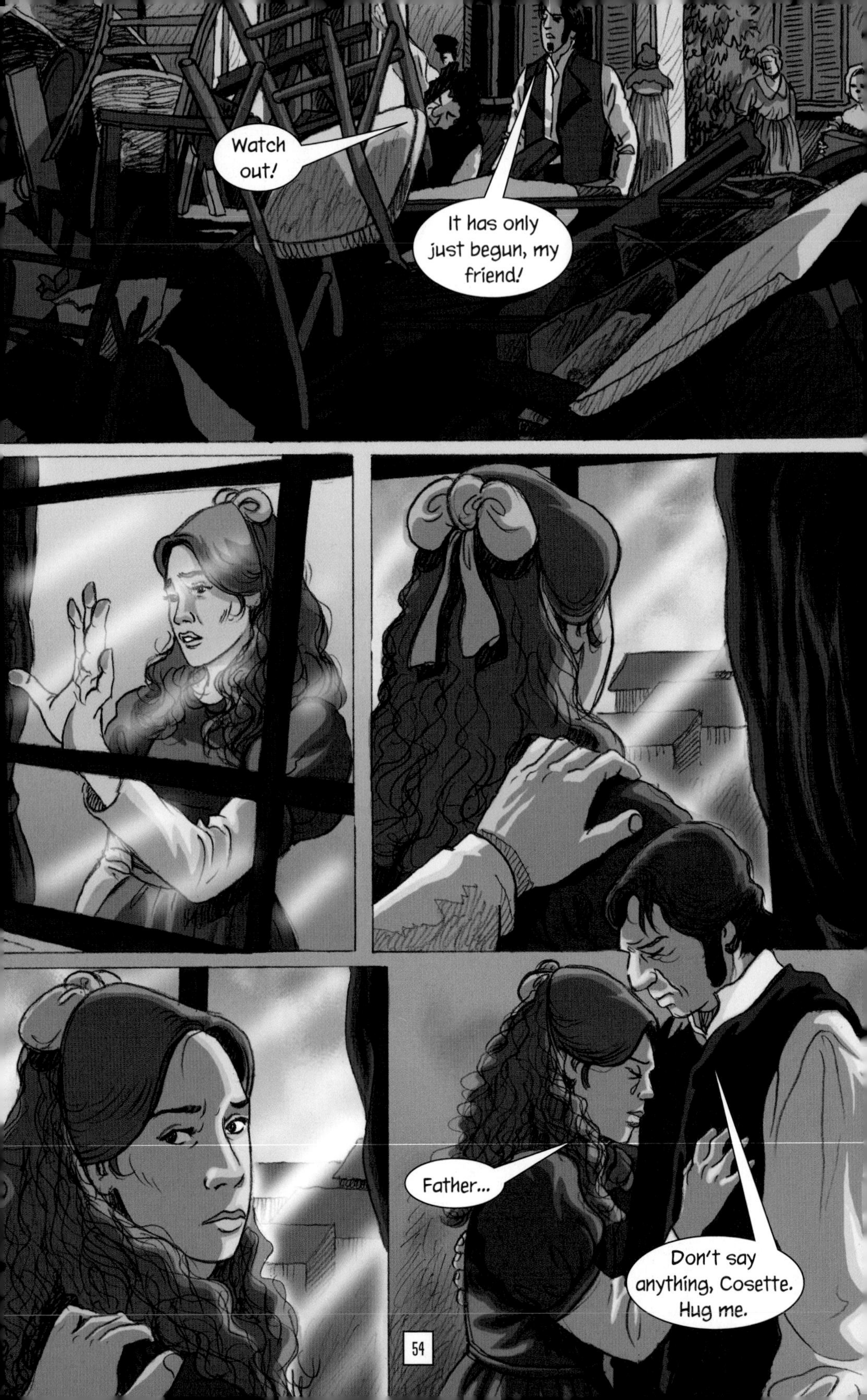

Watch out!
It has only just begun, my friend!
Father...
Don't say anything, Cosette. Hug me.

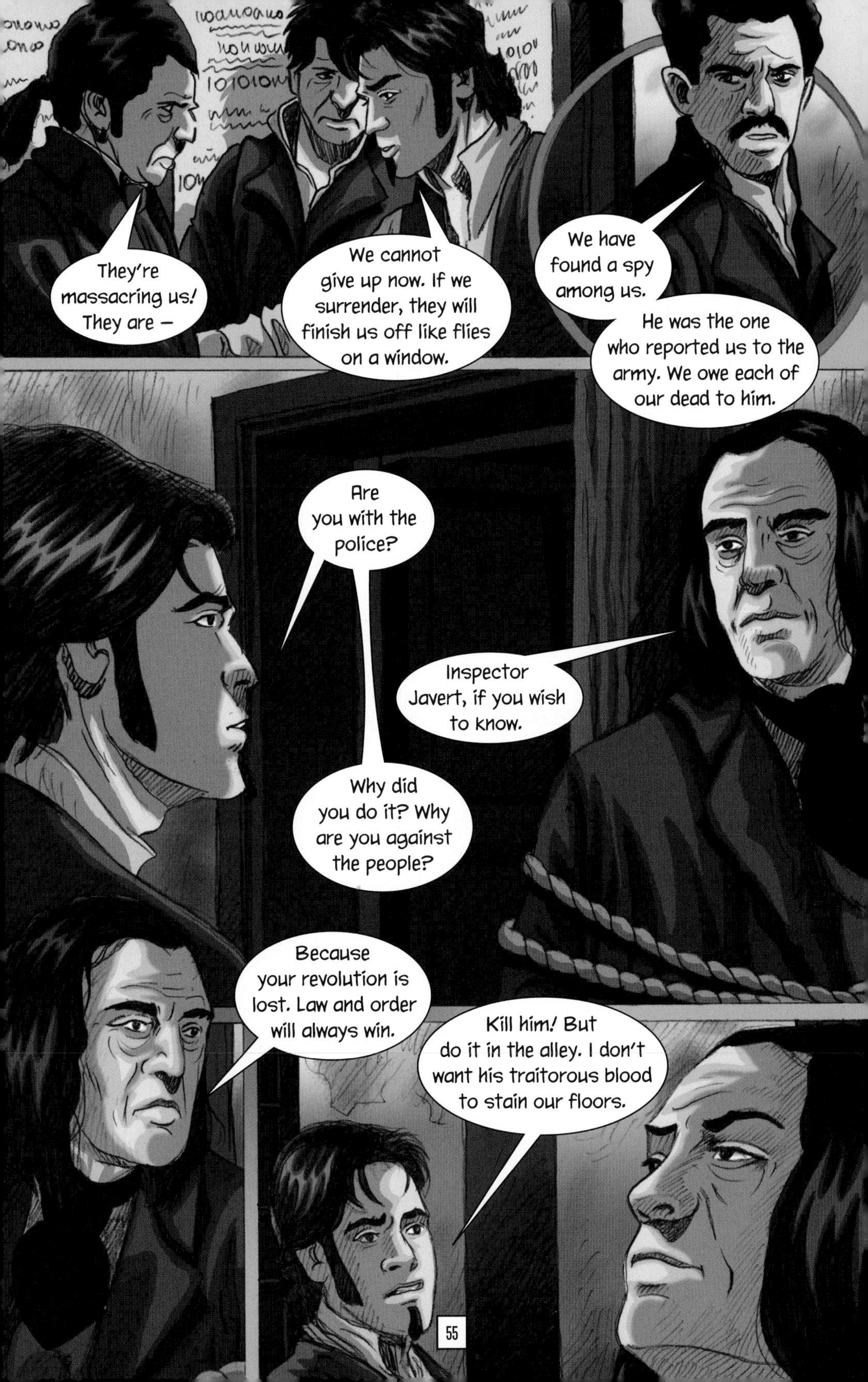
They're massacring us! They are –
We cannot give up now. If we surrender, they will finish us off like flies on a window.
We have found a spy among us.
He was the one who reported us to the army. We owe each of our dead to him.
Are you with the police?
Inspector Javert, if you wish to know.
Why did you do it? Why are you against the people?
Because your revolution is lost. Law and order will always win.
Kill him! But do it in the alley. I don't want his traitorous blood to stain our floors.

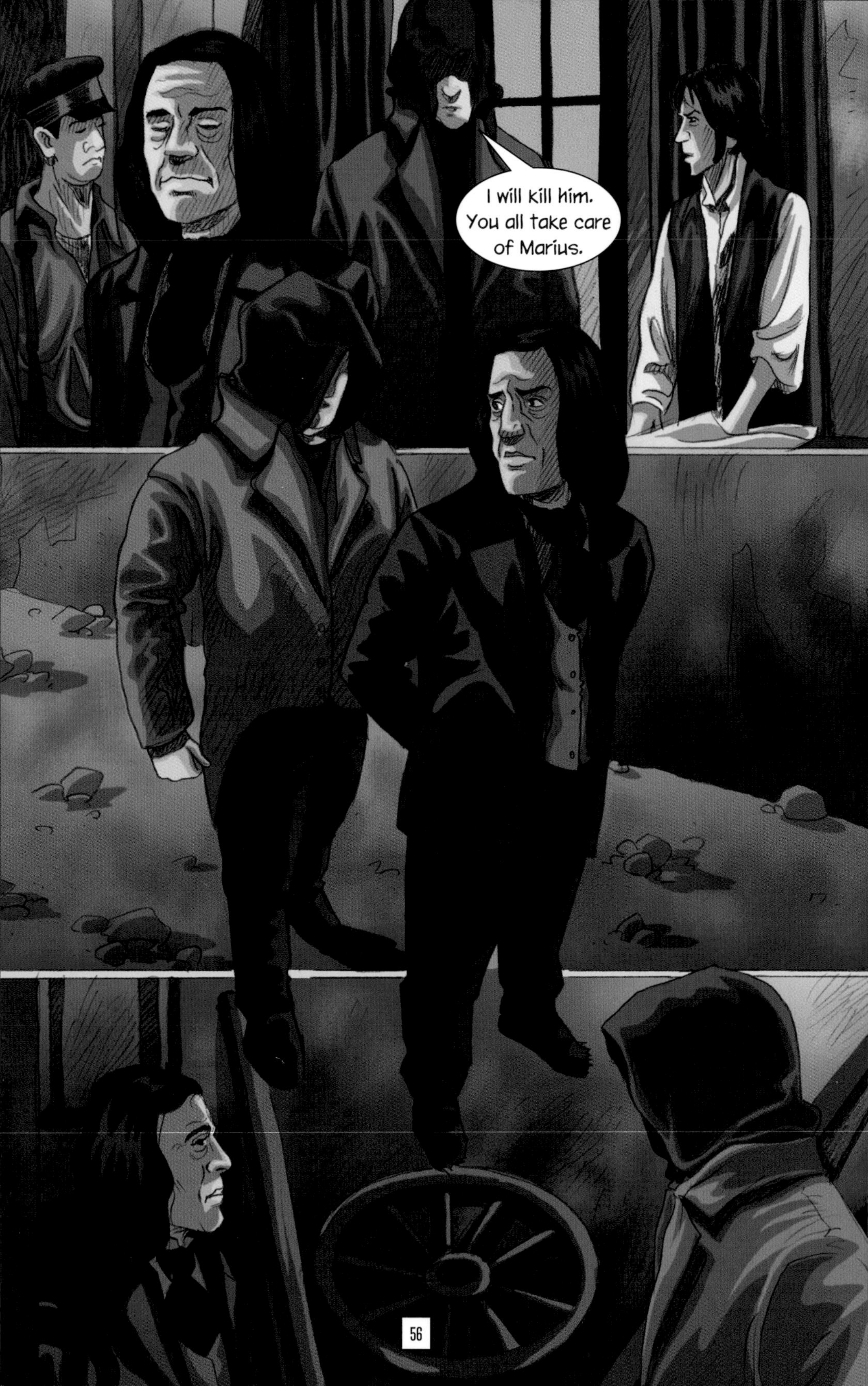
I will kill him. You all take care of Marius.

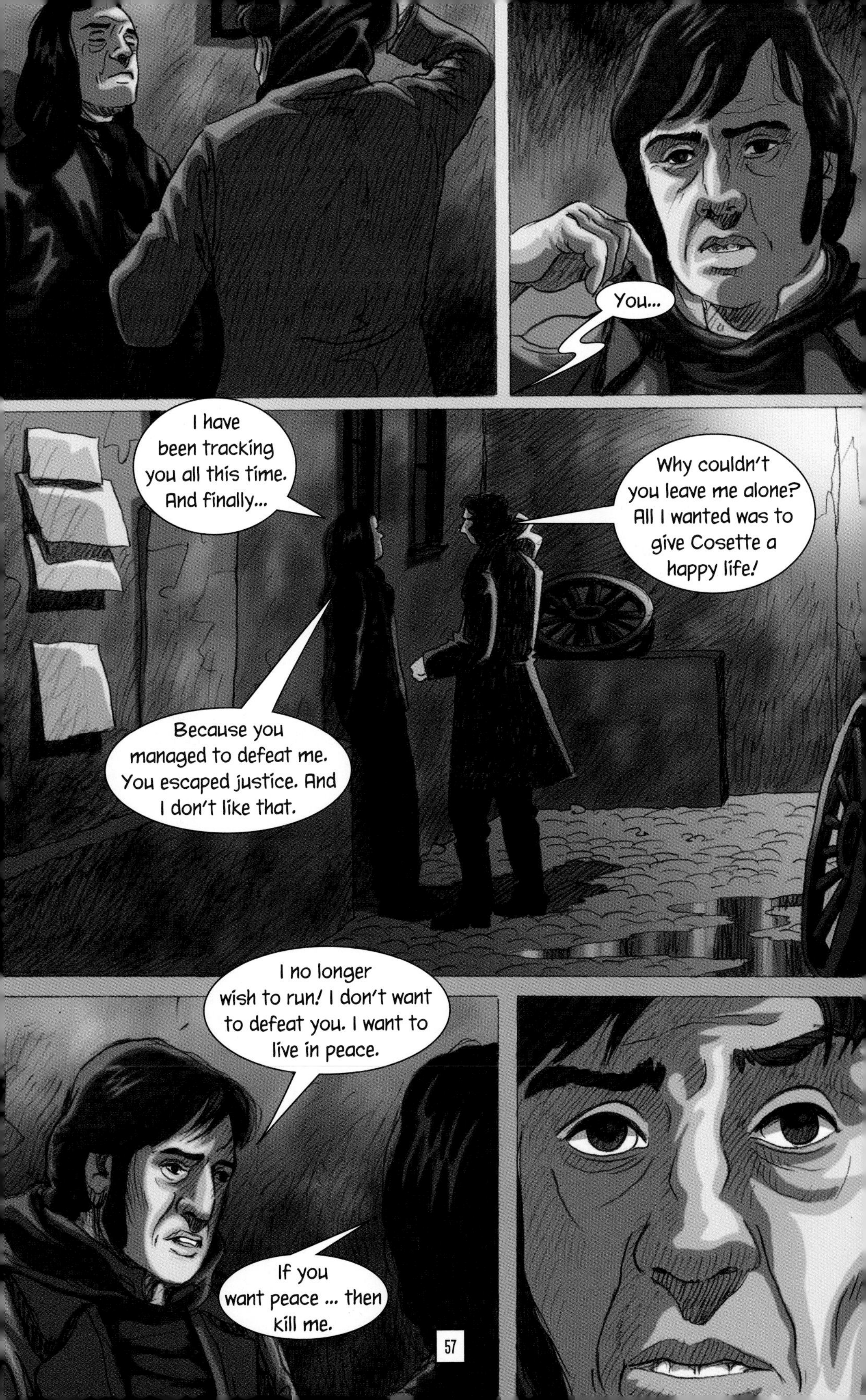
You...
I have been tracking you all this time. And finally...
Why couldn't you leave me alone? All I wanted was to give Cosette a happy life!
Because you managed to defeat me. You escaped justice. And I don't like that.
I no longer wish to run! I don't want to defeat you. I want to live in peace.
If you want peace ... then kill me.

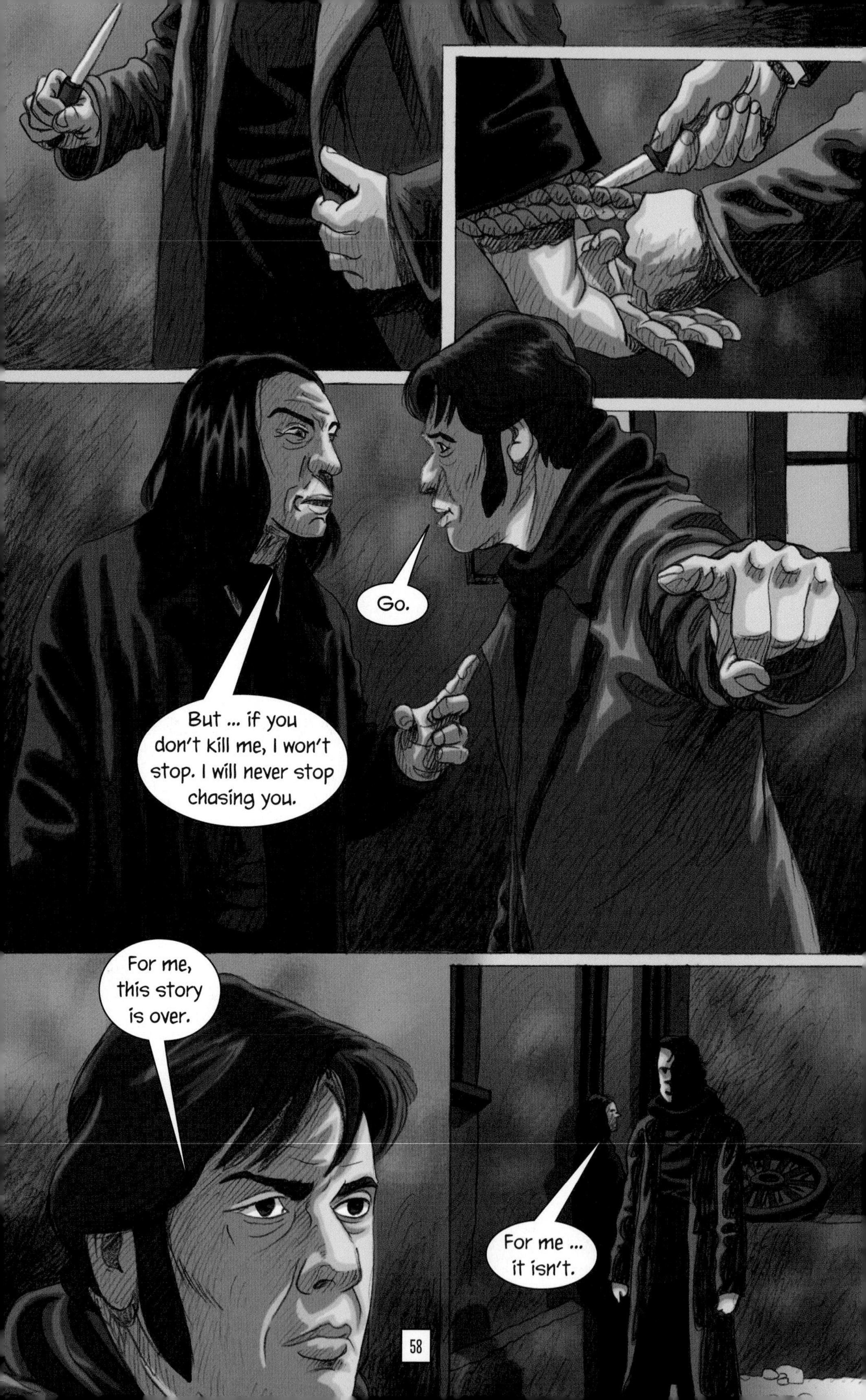
Go.
But ... if you don't kill me, I won't stop. I will never stop chasing you.
For me, this story is over.
For me ... it isn't.

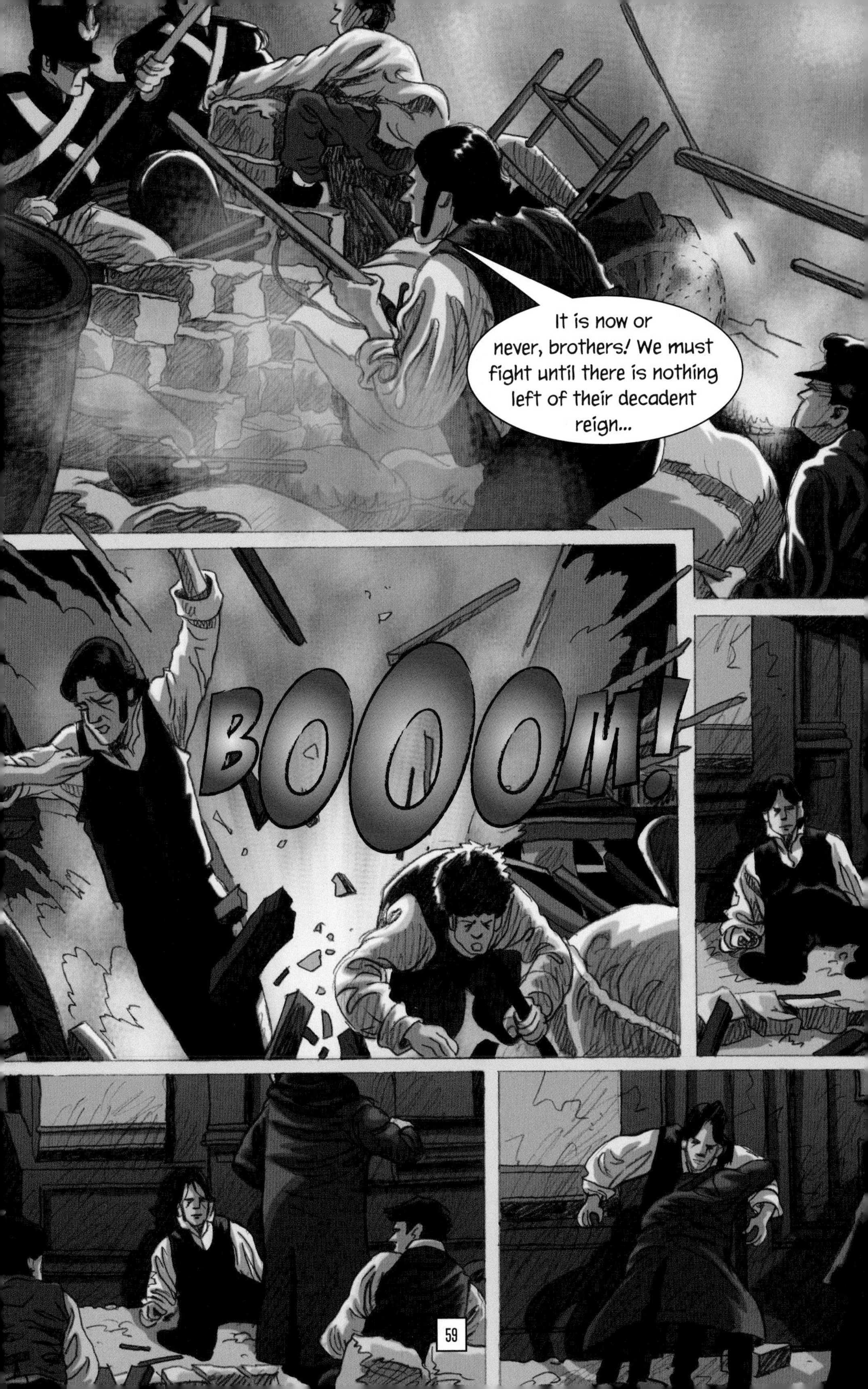
It is now or never, brothers! We must fight until there is nothing left of their decadent reign...
BOOOOM!

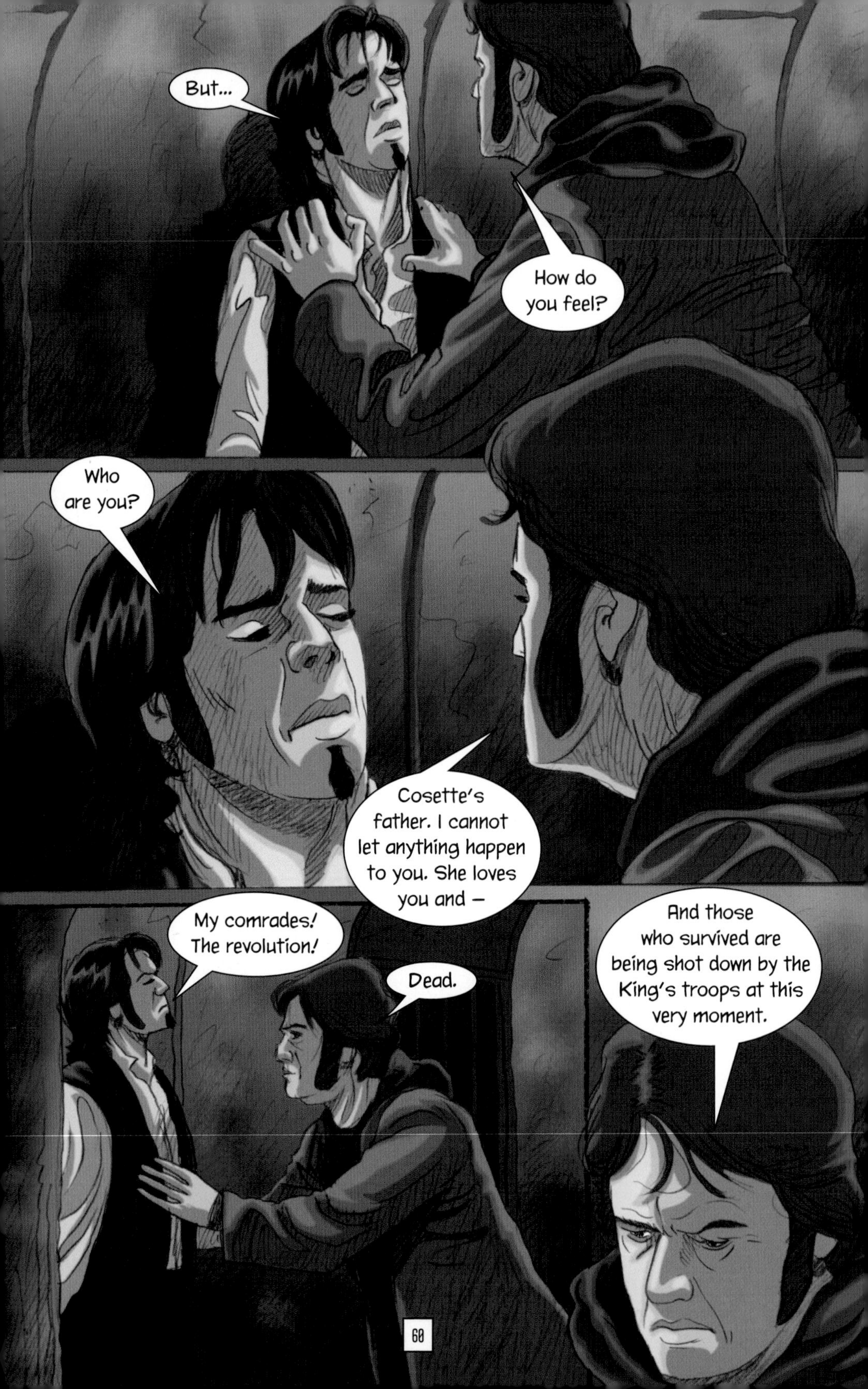
But...
How do you feel?
Who are you?
Cosette's father. I cannot let anything happen to you. She loves you and –
My comrades! The revolution!
Dead.
And those who survived are being shot down by the King's troops at this very moment.

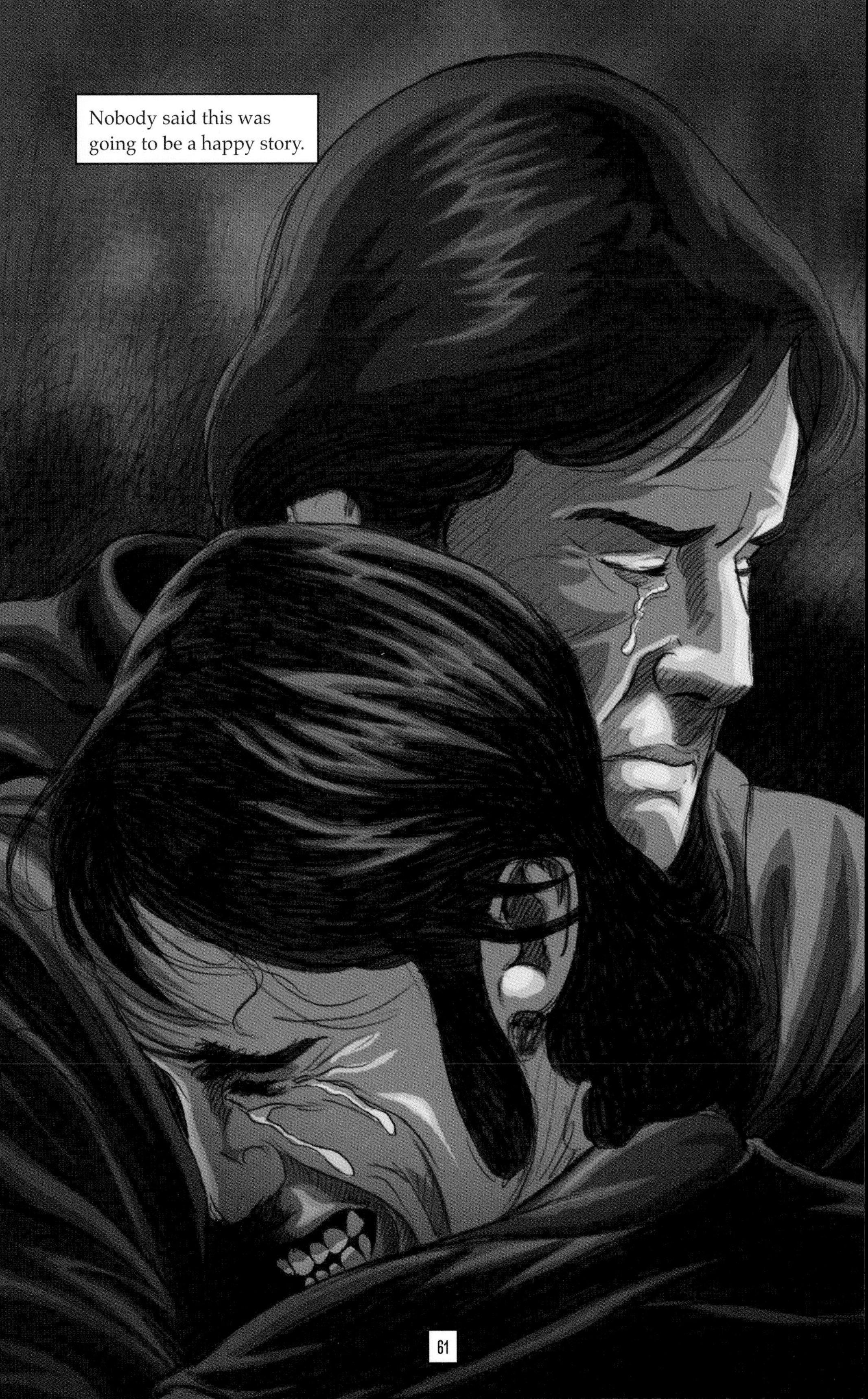
Nobody said this was going to be a happy story.

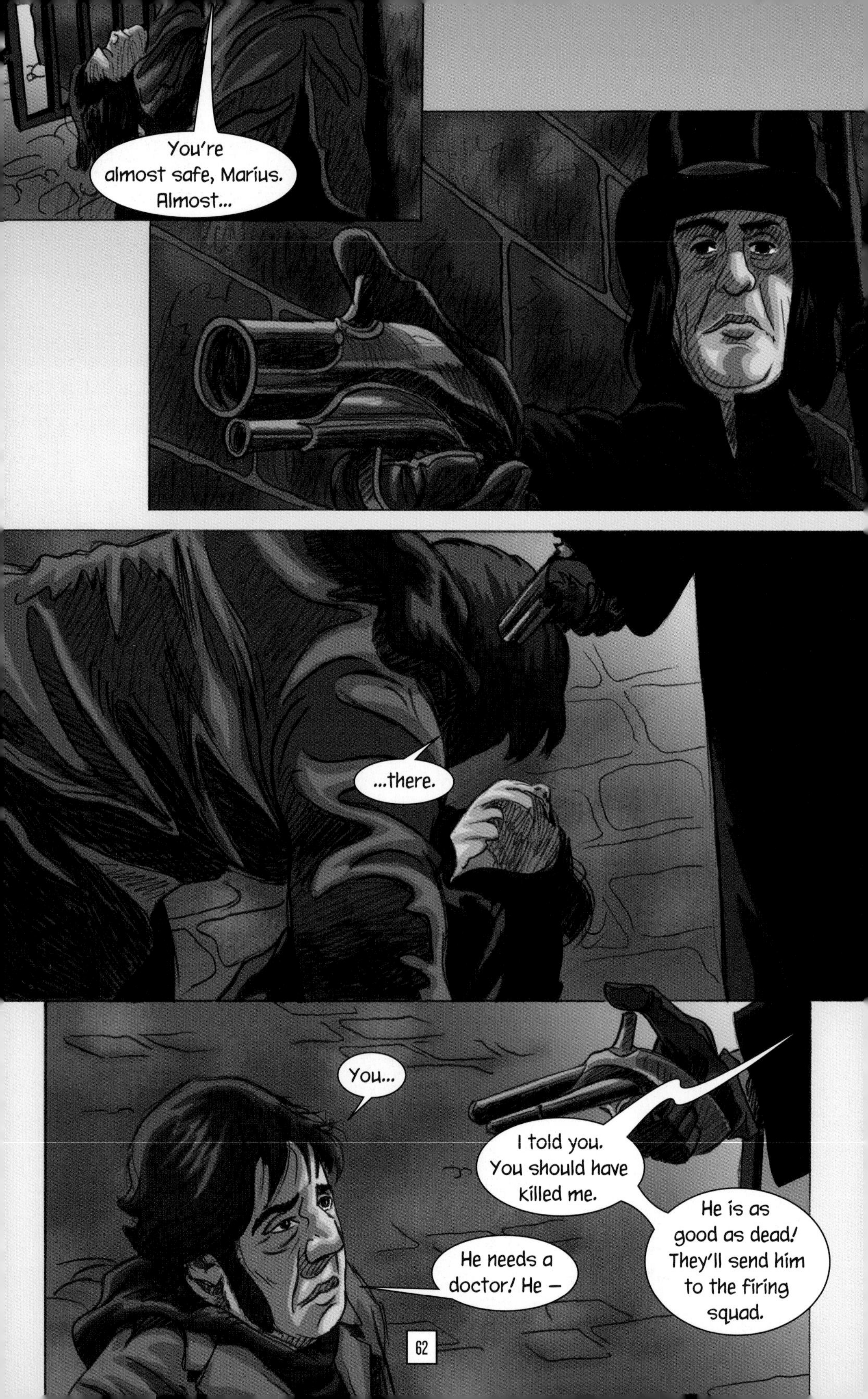
You're almost safe, Marius. Almost...
...there.
You...
I told you. You should have killed me.
He is as good as dead! They'll send him to the firing squad.
He needs a doctor! He –

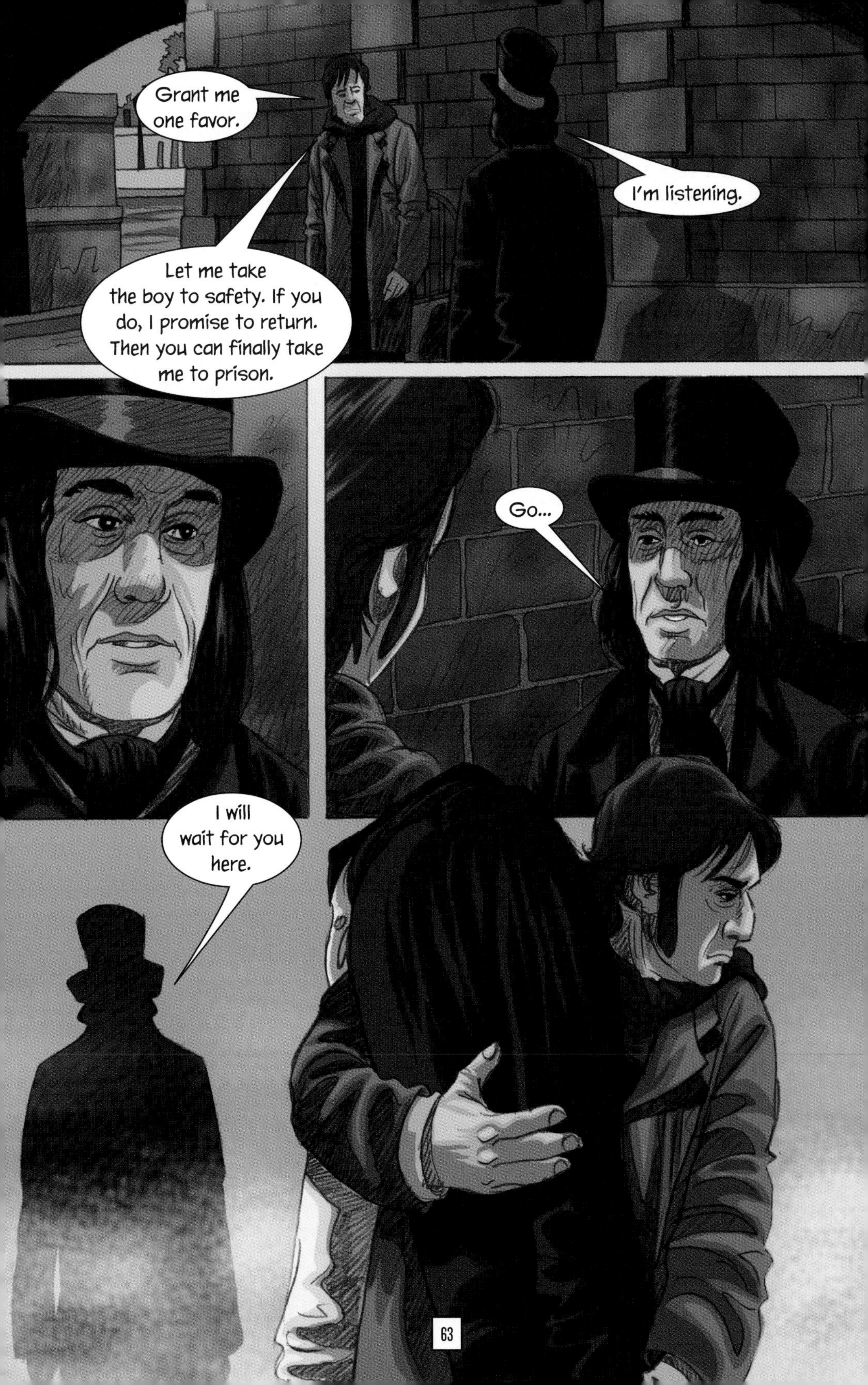
Grant me one favor.
I'm listening.
Let me take the boy to safety. If you do, I promise to return. Then you can finally take me to prison.
Go...
I will wait for you here.

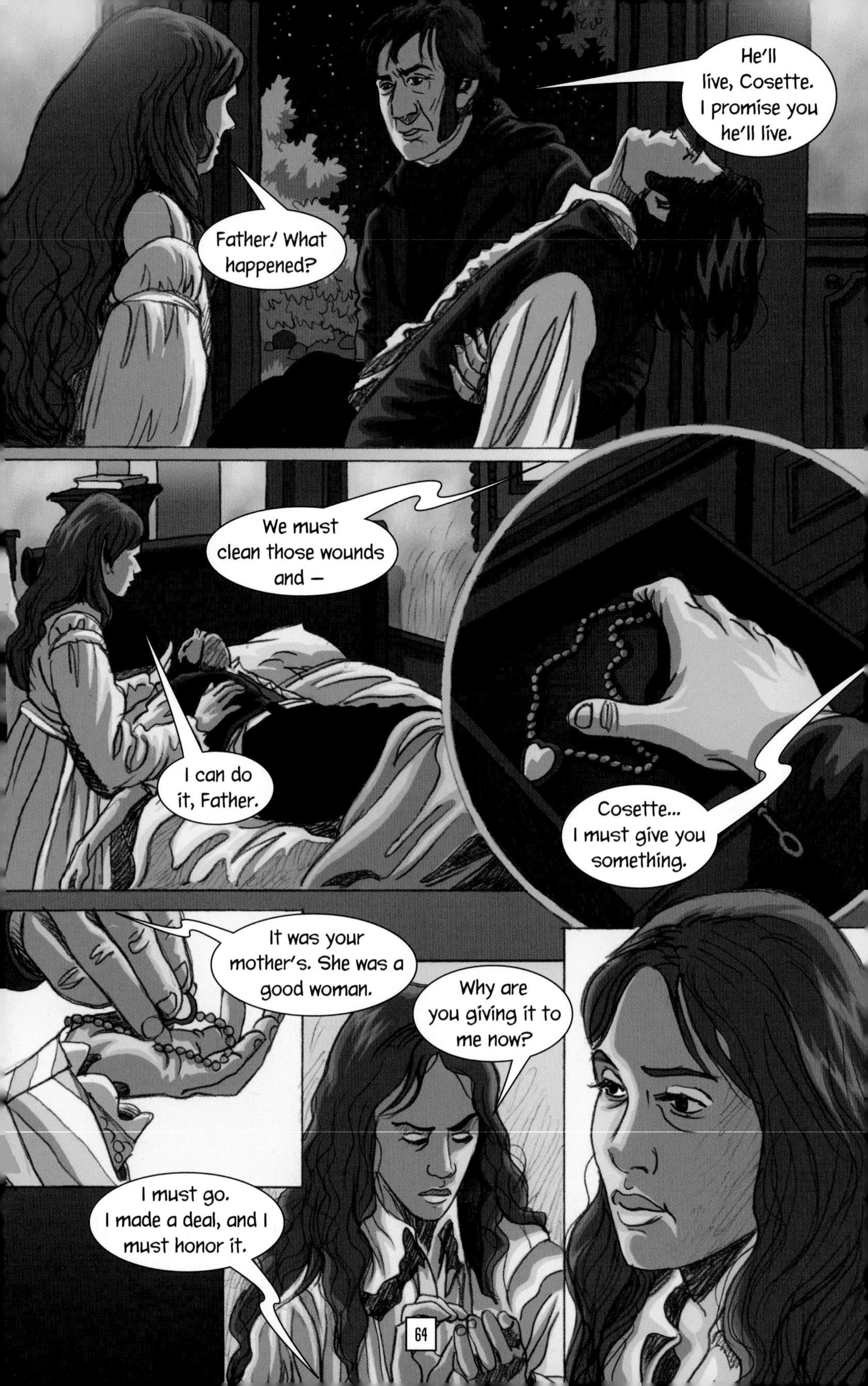
He'll live, Cosette. I promise you he'll live.
Father! What happened?
We must clean those wounds and –
I can do it, Father.
Cosette... I must give you something.
It was your mother's. She was a good woman.
Why are you giving it to me now?
I must go. I made a deal, and I must honor it.

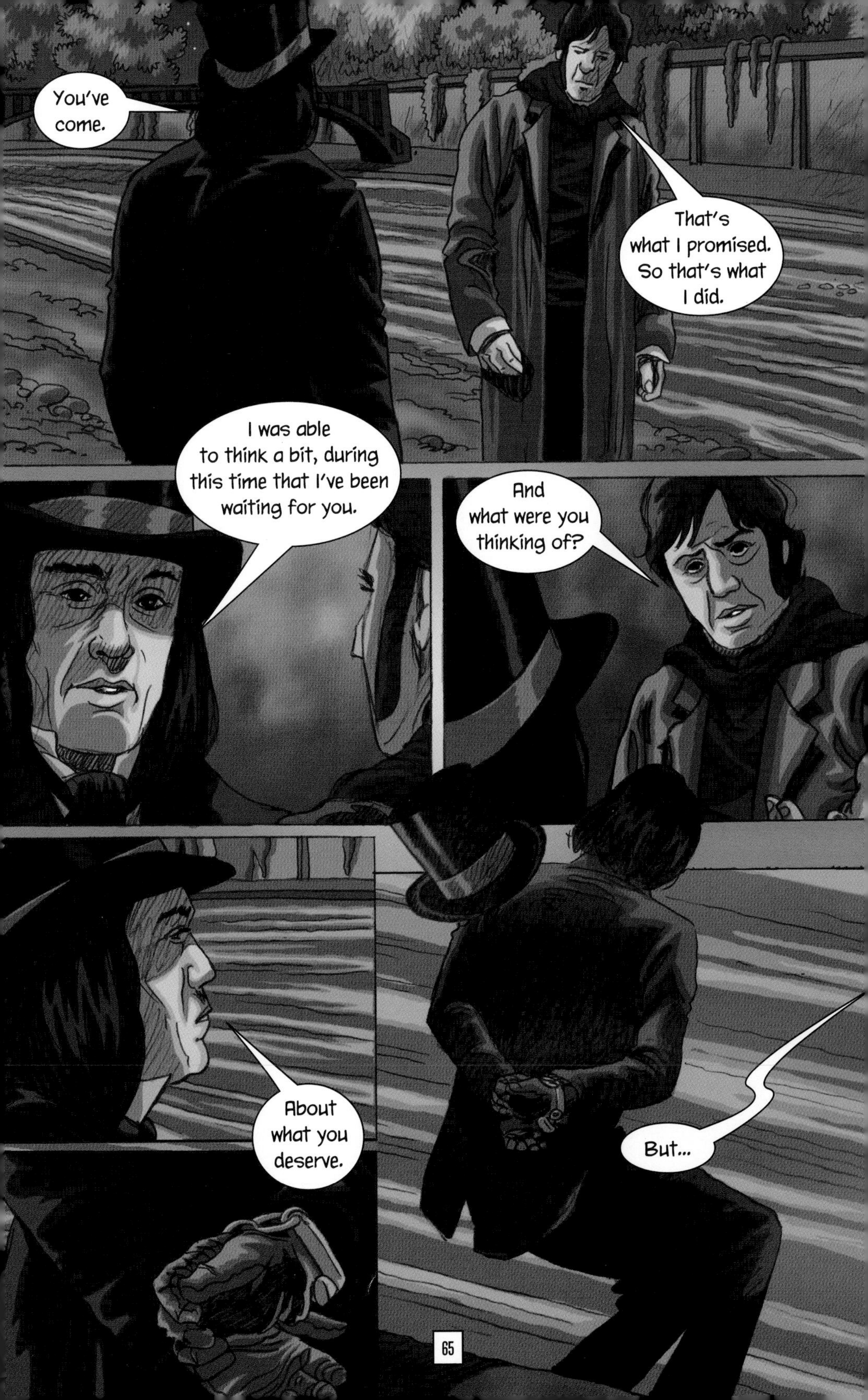
You've come.
That's what I promised. So that's what I did.
I was able to think a bit, during this time that I've been waiting for you.
And what were you thinking of?
About what you deserve.
But...

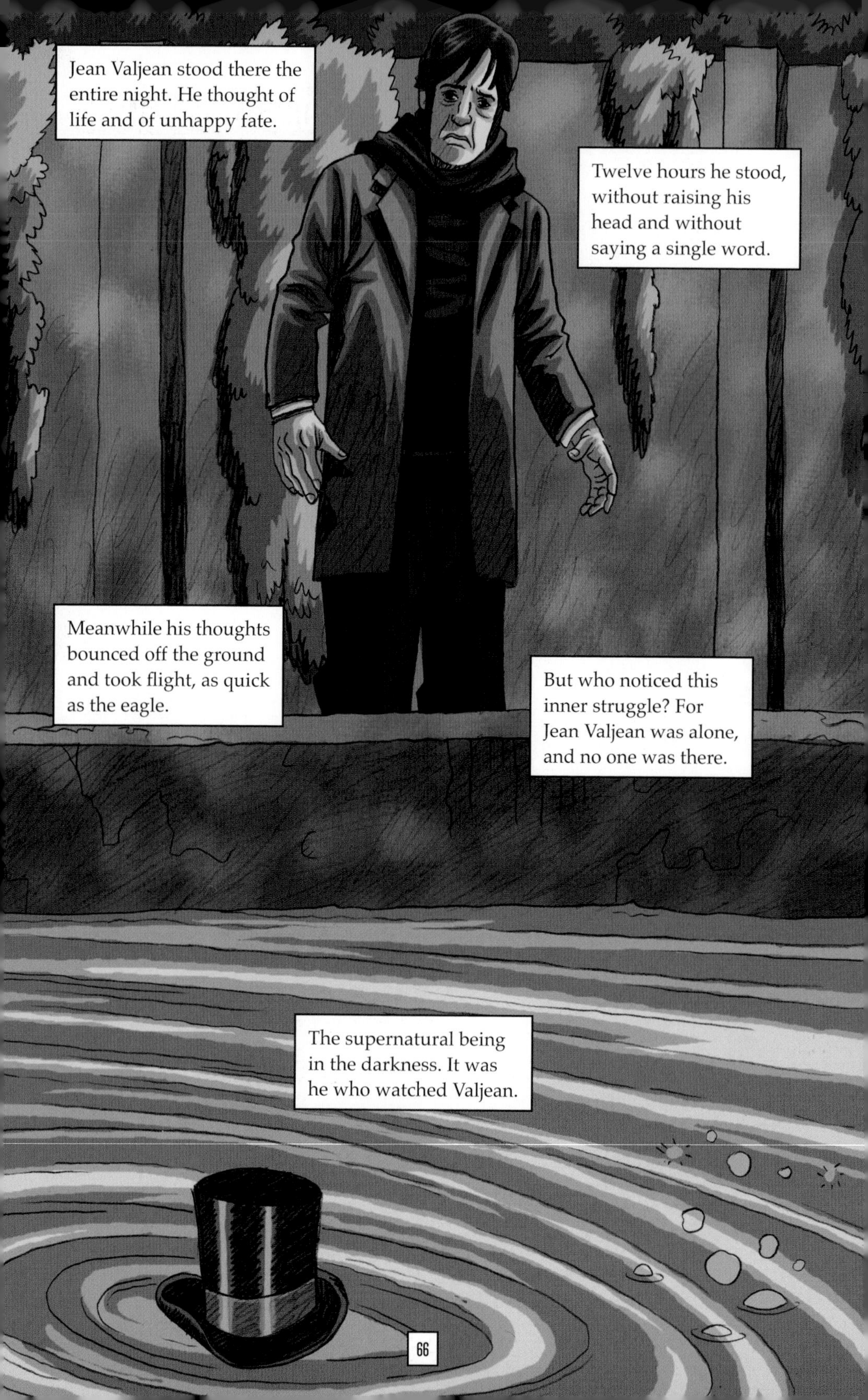
Jean Valjean stood there the entire night. He thought of life and of unhappy fate.
Twelve hours he stood, without raising his head and without saying a single word.
Meanwhile his thoughts bounced off the ground and took flight, as quick as the eagle.
But who noticed this inner struggle? For Jean Valjean was alone, and no one was there.
The supernatural being in the darkness. It was he who watched Valjean.

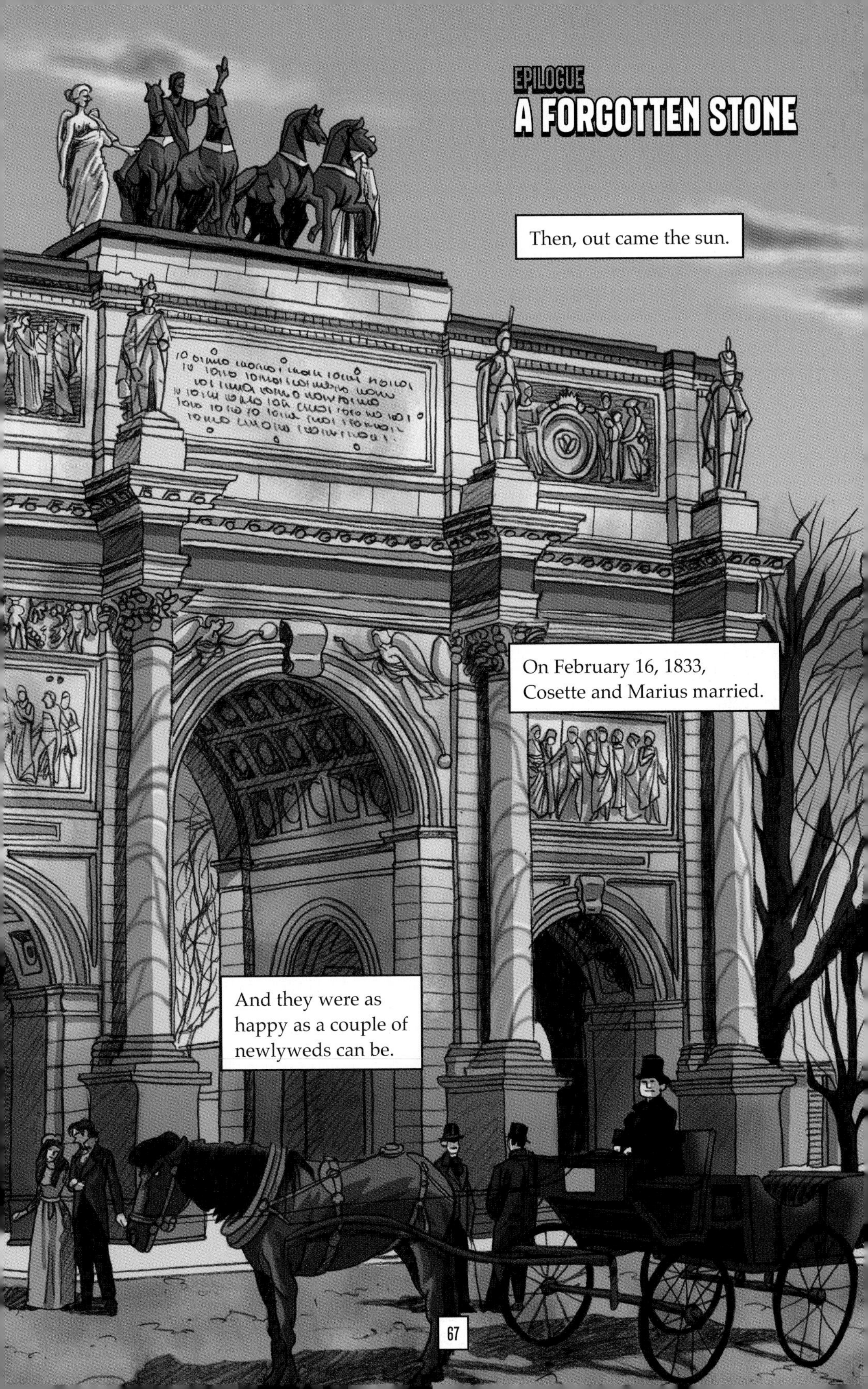
EPILOGUE
A FORGOTTEN STONE
Then, out came the sun.
On February 16, 1833, Cosette and Marius married.
And they were as happy as a couple of newlyweds can be.

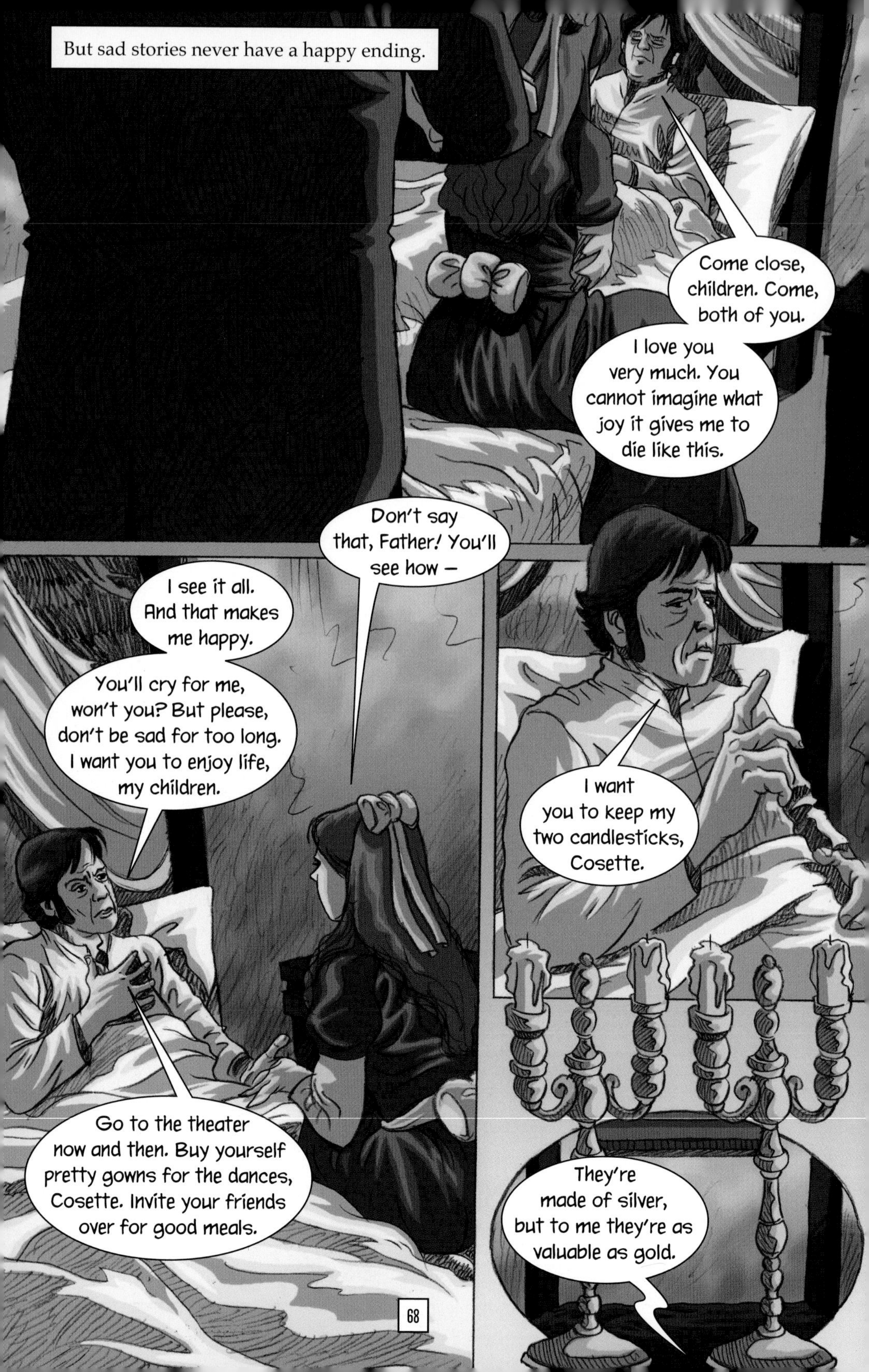

But sad stories never have a happy ending.
Come close, children. Come, both of you.
I love you very much. You cannot imagine what joy it gives me to die like this.
Don't say that, Father! You'll see how –
I see it all. And that makes me happy.
You'll cry for me, won't you? But please, don't be sad for too long. I want you to enjoy life, my children.
Go to the theater now and then. Buy yourself pretty gowns for the dances, Cosette. Invite your friends over for good meals.
I want you to keep my two candlesticks, Cosette.
They're made of silver, but to me they're as valuable as gold.

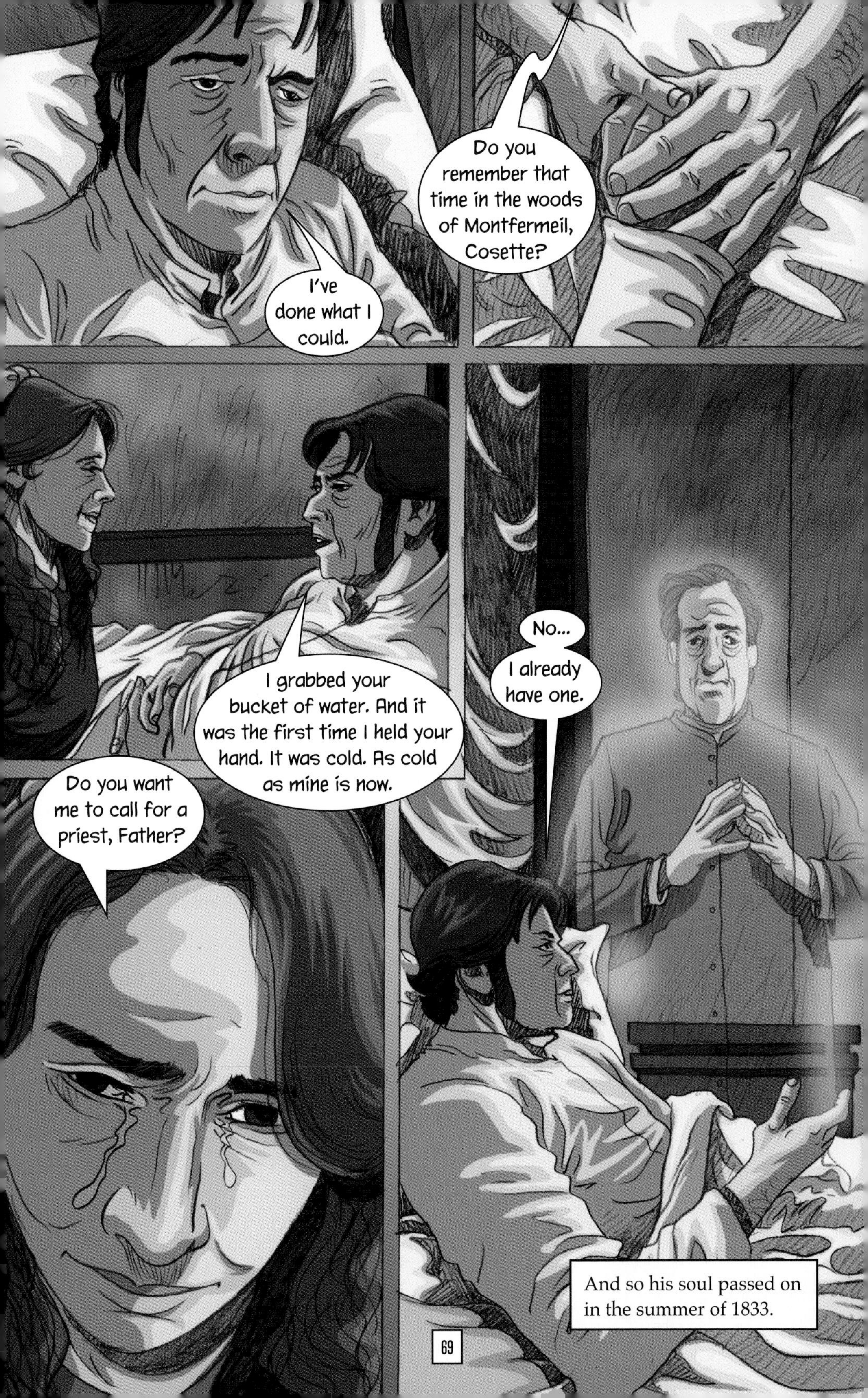
I've done what I could.
Do you remember that time in the woods of Montfermeil, Cosette?
I grabbed your bucket of water. And it was the first time I held your hand. It was cold. As cold as mine is now.
Do you want me to call for a priest, Father?
No...
I already have one.
And so his soul passed on in the summer of 1833.

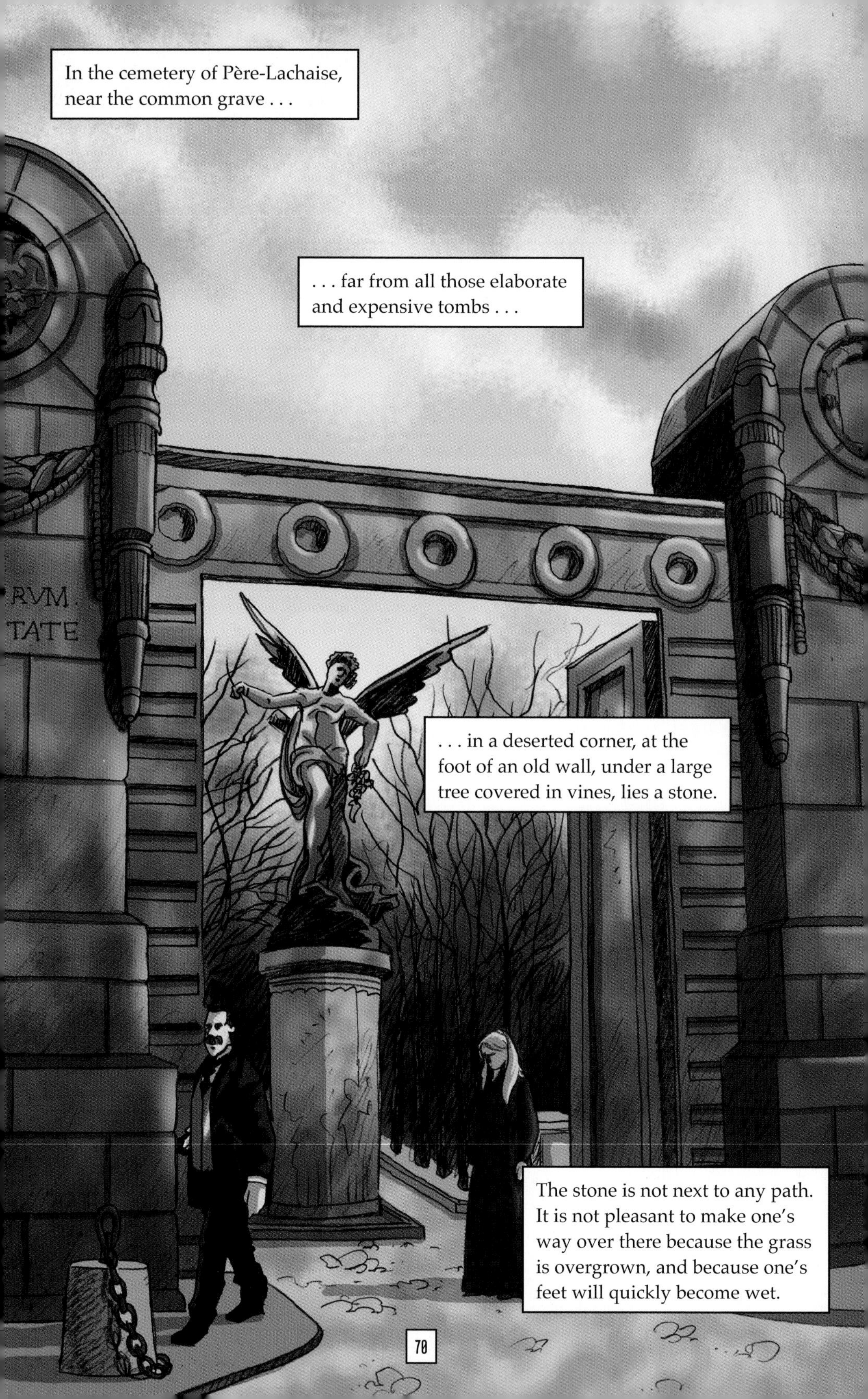
In the cemetery of Père-Lachaise, near the common grave . . .
. . . far from all those elaborate and expensive tombs . . .
RVM.
TATE
. . . in a deserted corner, at the foot of an old wall, under a large tree covered in vines, lies a stone.
The stone is not next to any path. It is not pleasant to make one's way over there because the grass is overgrown, and because one's feet will quickly become wet.

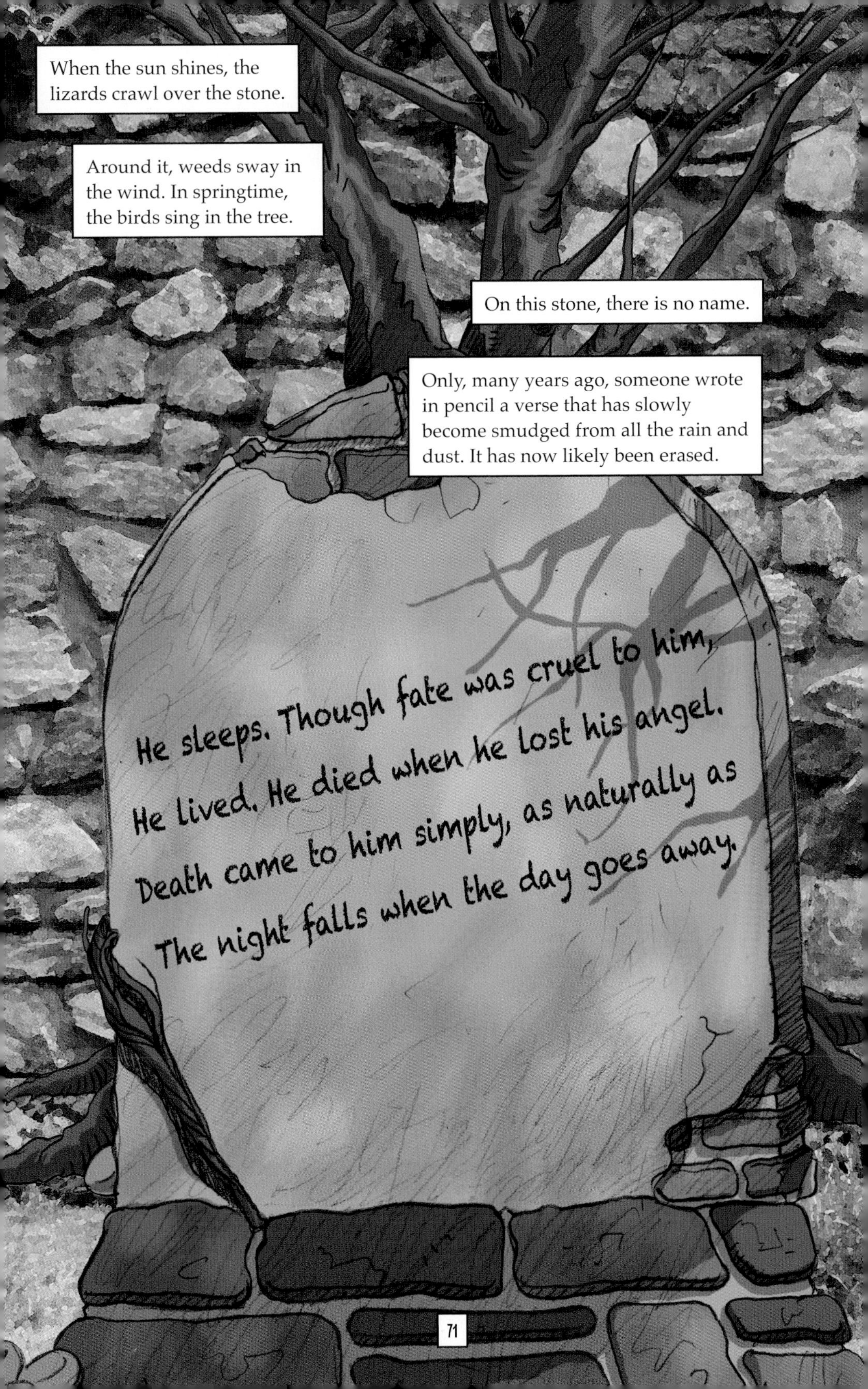
When the sun shines, the lizards crawl over the stone.
Around it, weeds sway in the wind. In springtime, the birds sing in the tree.
On this stone, there is no name.
Only, many years ago, someone wrote in pencil a verse that has slowly become smudged from all the rain and dust. It has now likely been erased.
He sleeps. Though fate was cruel to him,
He lived. He died when he lost his angel.
Death came to him simply, as naturally as
The night falls when the day goes away.

ABOUT THE AUTHOR

Victor Hugo was born in France, in 1802, and is considered to be one of France's greatest writers. He was a passionate supporter of Romanticism, a movement in the arts that emphasized emotion and individualism. In addition to being a novelist, Hugo was a poet and playwright, and he held political offices during the French Second Republic (1848–1852). In 1831 he published one of his most memorable novels, *Notre Dame de Paris* (*The Hunchback of Notre Dame*). Years later, in 1862, he published *Les Misérables*. This novel expressed many of his concerns regarding the poor social conditions in France during the first half of the 19th century. Hugo died in Paris, France, in 1885.

ABOUT THE RETELLING AUTHOR AND ILLUSTRATOR

Luciano Saracino (Buenos Aires, 1978) has had his works published in languages as diverse as Italian, French, Portuguese, English, Korean, Serbian, German, Greek, and Russian. He has written novels, screenplays for TV series, children's books, essays, song lyrics, and comics. Saracino is a member of the group Banda Dibujada, in which he participates in a number of activities that help bring comics to children.

Fabián Mezquita began to publish his work professionally in 1998. In 2001 he worked as an assistant to the comic book artist Carlos Meglia, to continue his career as an illustrator working for advertising agencies as well as various Argentine and foreign publishing houses. He is a founding and active member of Banda Dibujada, a group devoted to promoting the creation and reading of children's comics.

GLOSSARY

barricade (BAR-uh-kade)—a temporary thing set up to keep people from entering an area

convent (KON-vent)—a building where a group of religious women called nuns live

convict (KAHN-vikt)—someone who is or has been in prison for committing a crime

decadent (DEK-uh-duhnt)—having low morals and only interested in one's own money, fame, and other pleasures

foreigner (FOR-uhn-er)—someone who comes from somewhere else

fugitive (FYOO-juh-tiv)—someone who is running from the law

hypocrite (HIP-uh-krit)—a person whose actions go against what he or she claims to believe or feel

lark (LAHRK)—a small bird with brownish feathers that has a pleasant song

Monseigneur (mawn-se-NYOR)—a French title given to bishops, princes, and other important figures

republic (ri-PUHB-lik)—a kind of government where the people elect a small group of people to make decisions for the whole

revolution (rev-uh-LOO-shun)—a violent uprising by the people of a country that changes its system of government

strike (STRIKE)—the action of refusing to work because of an argument or a disagreement with an employer over wages or working conditions

superstition (soo-pur-STI-shuhn)—a belief or way of behaving that is based in ignorance or in fear of the unknown

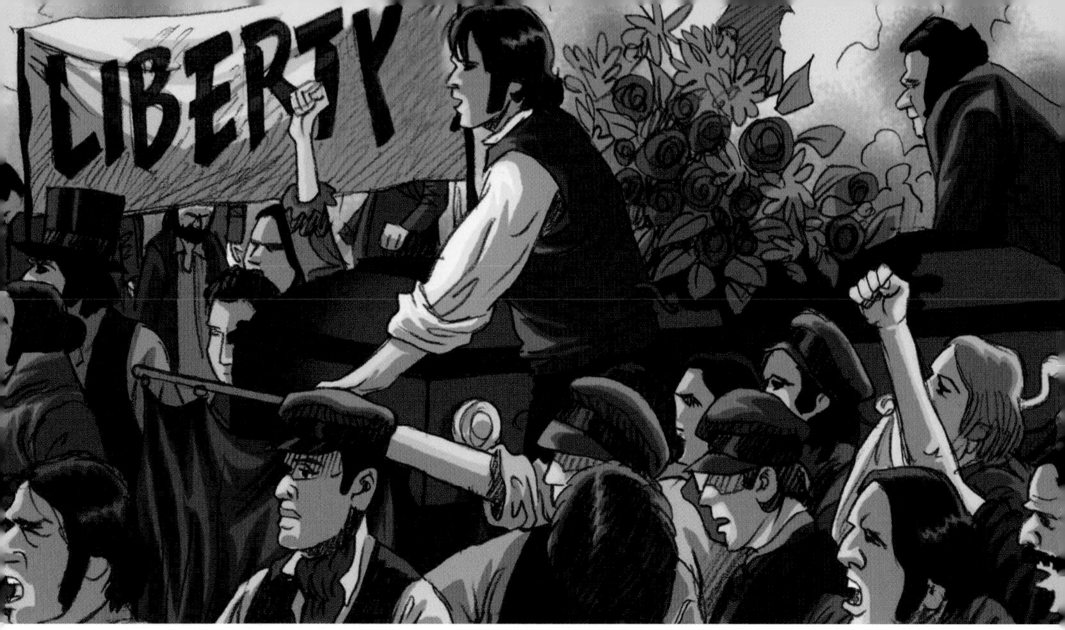
LIBERTY

THE CENTURY OF REVOLUTIONS

At the end of the 18th century, France began experiencing intense political unrest. *Les Misérables* is set during this period, which starts with the French Revolution in 1789, and ends in 1870 with the beginning of the Third Republic.

THE FRENCH REVOLUTION

At the close of the 18th century, France was governed by a monarchy. Louis XVI was king. Most of the country suffered from poverty and hunger. A new social class, the bourgeoisie, began to question the "divine right" of monarchs to rule. They put forward the ideals of liberty, equality, and fraternity. Revolution broke out with the storming of the Bastille on July 14, 1789. A few weeks later the palace of Versailles was taken. Louis XVI and his wife, Marie Antoinette, remained as king and queen, but they now shared power with a Legislative Assembly. But in 1793, after the so-called Second Revolution, the monarchs were executed. A period known as the Reign of Terror began. The Jacobins, an extremist group of revolutionaries, rose to power. In one year, they executed over ten thousand people accused of being against the revolution. In 1794, the Jacobin leader was overthrown. A new authority called the Directory governed France, until a general who had been a hero of the revolutionary war decided to take control. His name was Napoleon Bonaparte.

NAPOLEON'S EMPIRE

On November 9, 1799, Napoleon overthrew the government and set up his own. It was called the Consulate, and he held the position of First Consul. In 1804, Napoleon gained even more power when he was crowned Emperor of the French. While emperor, Napoleon invaded other European countries. It wasn't until 1815 that he was defeated at the Battle of Waterloo. Napoleon died in exile in 1821.

THE RESTORATION

After the fall of Napoleon, the monarchy returned to power. This period, known as the Restoration, included the reigns of Louis XVIII and Charles X. However, these were constitutional monarchies. The monarchs did not have absolute authority like before. But soon the lowest classes were worse off than before the revolution of 1789. In July of 1830, a great revolution overthrew Charles X and put Louis Philippe I of Orleans on the throne. In June of 1832, there was another revolt. The June Rebellion, which is the uprising narrated in *Les Misérables*, began on the day of the funeral of Lamarque, a republican general. It was over quickly, though. The rebellion ended the next day, with more than 150 people dead.

THE REVOLUTION OF 1848

Louis Philippe remained king until 1848, when a new revolution brought about the Second Republic. It seemed as if the original revolutionary ideals would once again rise to power. But in 1851, Napoleon's nephew, Louis Bonaparte, took control. He declared himself Emperor of the French in 1852, which started the Second Empire. This imperial reign would last until 1870, when the Third Republic began. The Third Republic government lasted until 1940. At last, France would have some stability.

DISCUSSION
QUESTIONS

1. At the beginning of the story, the priest did not report Valjean for stealing. Instead, he made sure Valjean also took the candlesticks. Why do you think he did this? Would you have done the same thing in that situation?

2. After firing Fantine from his factory, Valjean tries to help her. Why do you think he did this? Do you agree with his attitude?

3. Why do you think Inspector Javert is so focused on catching Valjean and bringing him to justice? How would you describe Javert's character? Discuss it with your classmates.

4. Do you think there is a villain in this story? If so, who do you think it is? Talk about it, and be sure to use examples from the story to support your answer.

WRITING
PROMPTS

1. Imagine what might have happened between the first part of the story and the moment when Valjean is living under the name Mister Madeleine. How did he become so respected? Write about it.

2. Pretend that you are a reporter for a newspaper, and you witness the chaotic uprising at Lamarque's funeral. Write a chronicle of the events.

3. The French title *Les Misérables* can be translated as "The Miserable Ones," "The Poor Ones," or "The Wretched." Why do think Hugo chose this title? Who are "the miserable ones" in the story? Write three paragraphs about it, using examples from the story to support your answer.

4. Imagine that you are Jean Valjean. Write a letter to the priest, thanking him for his help and kindness. How did the act affect you? Be sure to let the priest know what you've been doing since leaving his house.

LES MISÉRABLES AND THE MOVIES

Les Misérables is a beloved work of literature that has been adapted many times, both to film and theater. Even in the early days of film, *Les Misérables* attracted the attention of artists. The story was brought to life for the first time in a 1909 silent film that focuses on the fugitive Jean Valjean and the policeman Inspector Javert.

Over the years, adaptations have been made throughout the world. There are, of course, French films based on Hugo's novel, but there are also Mexican, Brazilian, Indian, and Egyptian films, as well as Japanese anime adaptations. One notable English-language movie is a 1998 version. It stars Liam Neeson in the role of Valjean and Geoffrey Rush as Javert. The novel has also been adapted for the small screen with a number of miniseries and made-for-TV movies.

Despite all the film versions, the adaptation that has brought Victor Hugo's work the most renown is the successful *Les Misérables* musical. The first showing was held in 1985, at the Barbican Centre in London. The musical was immediately popular and has gone on to break records around the globe for being one of the longest-running musicals. In 2012 a film adaptation of the musical was made, starring Hugh Jackman as Valjean and Russell Crowe as Javert. The movie was also a worldwide success, receiving eight Academy Award nominations. The continued interest in *Les Misérables* demonstrates that Hugo's tale remains just as relevant today as it was in his time.

READ THEM ALL!

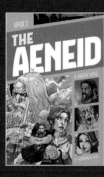

VIRGIL'S
THE AENEID
A GRAPHIC NOVEL

WILLIAM SHAKESPEARE'S
ROMEO AND JULIET
A GRAPHIC NOVEL

OSCAR WILDE'S
THE PICTURE OF DORIAN GRAY
A GRAPHIC NOVEL

HERMAN MELVILLE'S
MOBY DICK
A GRAPHIC NOVEL

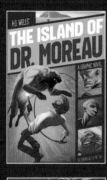

HG WELLS
THE ISLAND OF DR. MOREAU
A GRAPHIC NOVEL

EDGAR ALLAN POE'S
THE NARRATIVE OF ARTHUR GORDON PYM
A GRAPHIC NOVEL

HOMER'S
THE ILIAD
A GRAPHIC NOVEL

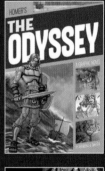

HOMER'S
THE ODYSSEY
A GRAPHIC NOVEL

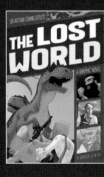

SIR ARTHUR CONAN DOYLE'S
THE LOST WORLD
A GRAPHIC NOVEL

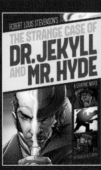

ROBERT LOUIS STEVENSON'S
THE STRANGE CASE OF DR. JEKYLL AND MR. HYDE
A GRAPHIC NOVEL

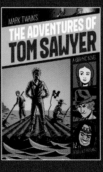

MARK TWAIN'S
THE ADVENTURES OF TOM SAWYER
A GRAPHIC NOVEL

BRAM STOKER'S
DRACULA
A GRAPHIC NOVEL

JULES VERNE'S
AROUND THE WORLD IN 80 DAYS
A GRAPHIC NOVEL

DANIEL DEFOE'S
ROBINSON CRUSOE
A GRAPHIC NOVEL

ANNA SEWELL'S
BLACK BEAUTY
A GRAPHIC NOVEL

VICTOR HUGO'S
THE HUNCHBACK OF NOTRE DAME
A GRAPHIC NOVEL

JOHANN DAVID WYSS

THE SWISS FAMILY ROBINSON

A GRAPHIC NOVEL

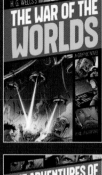

H. G. WELLS

THE WAR OF THE WORLDS

A GRAPHIC NOVEL

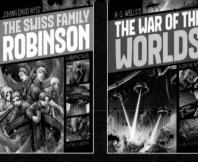

PERSEUS AND MEDUSA

A GRAPHIC NOVEL

THE ADVENTURES OF HERCULES

A GRAPHIC NOVEL

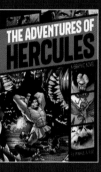

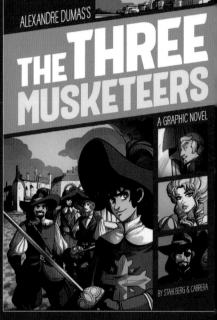

ALEXANDRE DUMAS'S

THE THREE MUSKETEERS

A GRAPHIC NOVEL

BY STAHLBERG & CABRERA

KENNETH GRAHAME'S

THE WIND IN THE WILLOWS

A GRAPHIC NOVEL

BY PETERS & CANO

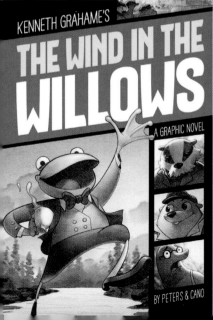

LEWIS CARROLL'S

ALICE IN WONDERLAND

A GRAPHIC NOVEL

JONATHAN SWIFT'S

GULLIVER'S TRAVELS

A GRAPHIC NOVEL

H.G. WELLS

THE TIME MACHINE

J.M. BARRIE'S

PETER PAN

A GRAPHIC NOVEL